THE AUGUSTINIAN
CORRESPONDENCE

THE AUGUSTINIAN CORRESPONDENCE

A Novella in Seven Letters

KATHRYN PURNELL

J R Garran

CONTENTS

Title: The Augustinian Correspondence

Author: Kathryn Purnell (1911-2006)

First published in 2018 as an eBook
First Printing 2020

ISBN 978-0-6488606-0-0

A Catalogue Entry for this book is available from The National Library of Australia

www.trove.nla.gov.au

'Joy is too exquisite, sorrow too bitter
to be borne alone'

Old Proverb.

PROLOGUE

'First, you must tell me why you ask for the letters.'

'Because as soon as Ru heard his father had the posting to Istanbul, nothing, but nothing, would change his mind about going there for the summer break. He'd promised to go to Scotland with me. It was all arranged. So we quarrelled and shouted rotten things at each other. No way would Ru give in. He said I could go with him or he'd go alone. Never mind Mummy, or me, or anybody else!'

'He must have given you a reason, dear.'

'Oh, some stuff about his grandfather and himself. Ru was only about three when his grandfather died – only three. It's incredible.'

Joanna realised her voice was growing shrill. She didn't want to lose her cool. Looking up, she was startled again by the coppery grey mass of hair surrounding the older woman's head. It almost looked like an afro and made her face seem small and soft. Not like Ru's mother, whose same hair somehow emphasised the bone structure of her face and made her seem severely Establishment. Ru's mother had been quiet at first, even stiff at the very time she was most charming. Joanna hadn't found her easy, the opposite in fact, which made her feel right up against the generation gap. Here with Ru's grandmother, whom she'd met only once before, she was beginning to feel equally uneasy. She bit her lip to control her temper.

Then, inexplicably, she thought of her own grandfather, precise, sour, always wiser than expected and inevitably polite, these character-

1

istics accentuated since his knighthood. Joanna smiled. She adored her grandfather. 'Actually my grandfather sent me,' she confided, surprising herself. 'After I broke it off with Ru I was moping around and he told me off, demanded to know if I'd fallen in love intelligently this time. I burst into tears and he gave me a tissue and really listened for once when I told him about Ru. Then he floored me by asking if Ru's grandmother was still alive: "Do you know his grandmother, the one who lives here, near Regents Park"?

'I just gasped. I could scarcely believe it but he began to chuckle. I hadn't seen him so amused since he retired and that's the truth. He walked over to the cabinet, got himself a whisky and stood there with his back to me muttering, "coincidence, unbelievable, unbelievable". He didn't even offer me a drink so I knew he'd been bowled. Finally he turned around and said to me, "Joanna, if you really want that boy, go and ask his grandmother to let you read the Augustinian correspondence. If you don't love him don't go".'

'So you really love Ru?'

Joanna lifted her head and stared straight into the older woman's eyes, still large and blue, with their own sparkle of humour and the demand for truth.

'Yes, I do,' Joanna said.

'Then I'll go and get the letters. I wrote the first myself

THE
CORRESPONDENCE

The Letter to Thomas

You and I had a ridiculous situation on which to base our new relationship. Had this not been so, perhaps I would not have been able to muster the courage to write this letter. Helena's voice comes to me new, strident with excitement as she ran in and out of every room in the house. 'He's here, darling. The plane was early. Thomas is here.'

And there you were, standing on the front doorstep, a little embarrassed, perhaps, at the lack of reception on the important occasion of your presentation as the most important person in Helena's life. You turned your face back towards the garden to be confronted first by an upturned basket of fruit and then by the descending feet of a red-haired woman in shorts slithering out of an apricot tree.

'You can't,' you said, 'you can't be—'

But I was. The boys had not picked the apricots as they promised before Peter took all four of them out of the way to give me the first hour with you and Helena. You did not know that I wished to display the first picking of our home-grown fruit on the tea table, carefully arranged for your welcome. The measure of you was your laughter as you stooped to pick up the apricots before you put your finger to your lips and returned to the front verandah, whistling to allow me time to enter the house from the back.

Helena discovered me in the kitchen. 'Oh, darling, you were hiding because we are early and caught you in your shorts. Never mind. He's at the front. Go on, get into your dress. I want you to look beautiful. Hurry up.'

Five minutes then, to change into the white dress I had laid out so carefully on the bed and then I was officially presented to you. With such pride, Thomas, such pride in us both.

'Here he is. Darling, this is Thomas.'

You rose grandly to the occasion. 'And just as charming as I expected,' you said.

You were putting me at my ease and I knew Helena loved you for saying what you did. She is so generous. It is her greatest quality, in spite of a life during which she has never been able to predict the next move.

You see, Thomas, to find me up a tree instead of in my proper place was not unusual, whereas for me to discover your acceptance was like rain on spring grass. I have always been capricious, but the thought that Helena should suffer for it in any but a minor way would shatter the very meaning of my life.

Like Helena, I have a happy disposition and I cannot depart from this personality trait even when the roots of it are shattered. I discovered this when I was a girl the age of Helena and now this knowledge often accounts for any selfish impulsiveness when happiness is threatened.

My parents were happy people in whom daily contentment glowed like a lamp. When I was a girl in Istanbul our family business was prosperous enough to keep us all in luxury without pretension. Father was one of those Englishmen, meticulous and careful, yet generous, who lived abroad by choice after the First World War. Mother, whose parents were émigré Russians, had been educated in England and finished by 'The Grand Tour', which included Istanbul and beyond. Both my parents adored Turkey and especially the 'most beautiful city in the world' where they lived a life of gaiety and culture.

When Father died, the year I commenced boarding school in England, he left us adequately provided for in a way that supported his business of harness equipment until my brother should come of age. Except for the journeys that took me back and forth to school, my mother continued to enjoy her life among the small intimate circle of her friends in

Istanbul. Respected by all, she had no desire to change her residence or her pattern of life. Times were difficult for the Turks during my childhood, but we seemed unaffected.

When my mother died suddenly of typhoid, I was eighteen. She had been busily preparing to take me on my own grand tour of Europe, during which, no doubt, she had expected I too would find my destiny in a good marriage.

I am telling you all this because it has somehow become important for the introduction of my request. I have come to the conclusion that it is not good enough that I make excuses to you, as I have to others when I am asked why I have not, and will not, return to Istanbul. You and Helena are together now, planning your marriage in the city of my heart. The city of the glorious skyline, tinted in the colours of moonlight and faded rose. There is a truth in Istanbul that I cannot deny Helena. There is also a force in the city that would deny her this truth forever.

The house of my childhood in Istanbul is no longer happy. My brother inhabits the premises with wealth. He has informed me, and perhaps you, that he intends to ensure for Helena a financial security that will completely establish her independence. You will already know that my brother paid for Helena's education in my old school in England and that he has been extraordinarily generous to her. He has made this effort to make up for what he considers to be the vicissitudes of her home life.

You are young and will think her uncle's wealth will make little difference to you and Helena, for you most certainly do not appear the kind of man to whom an heiress has double appeal. As for Helena, her character is such that money is no more than minor consideration. Helena loves you with the true sincerity of one who intends to share a life together. If I am not mistaken, this is also your most faithful intention. If I felt sure that my brother's intention was equally honourable, this letter would be unnecessary. Wealth in itself is neutral, but the uses of it can be open to question.

My brother has written to me in a manner that uses his money as a threat. It is possible that because of this, Helena may unknowingly sacrifice a right that could be of infinitely greater importance to her. The key to this right is mine, but it is known to no one else except my brother.

My mother used to say that happiness had to learn to live with its opposite. There was a Slavic fatalism in her character that accepted the personality of a son in whom true happiness seemed impossible. But I could not live without happiness. This was why, against my brother's wishes, I insisted on my grand tour after my mother's death and made the house in Istanbul no more than a temporary resting place to which I returned like a homing pigeon.

At first I was happier in the city of minarets than anywhere else on Earth. For my brother there was only unhappiness in a house he would not abandon. During the war, after I was widowed for the first time, he tried encourage me to come back with Helena. Not until this day have I questioned the obstinacy of my refusal.

You know the story of my life, how I ran away to China after the war to marry again. My second husband was a foreign correspondent who was infamous for irresponsibility long before I left him. Not that Helena would tell you in this manner. Her version would be that I returned from Shanghai having refused, as the mother of small twin sons, to travel to Chungking. She knows I loved Greg, who was good, but who never stayed long enough in one place to own the furniture or pay the bills, so that I understood soon enough that I would be responsible for the education of the children and would have to live in a reasonable place to earn the money to do it. Greg agreed in his heart but couldn't give up Chungking, though he sent me whatever funds he could for our home in England, to which part of him longed to return.

I managed well enough until he was killed. After that, I put the children into boarding school and worked full time, modelling clothes in a woman's world. But my reasons were not just financial. When I married Peter I had proved I could support myself and was safe. This may sound strange to you but the woman you met under the apricot tree was really me. I am fundamentally domestic and with Peter and my two boys and his two, I am truly happy. Because of this I am desperately anxious that Helena will be equally happy with you.

Because Helena was to visit you in Istanbul, I wrote to my brother concerning a friend from our youth. My question was simple: I asked no more than whether this friend still lived. My brother's answer by telegram amazed me, but the letter he sent after it was astounding.

He offered me a sum of money to refrain from involving Helena in my enquiry and threatened to disinherit Helena from a fortune if I persisted. The amount of money my brother mentioned seemed incredible to me, for though my brother is an astute businessman, he has never moved in the financial circles that promote such wealth and initially could only have based his investments on the profits of a business that modern automation forced into redundancy.

I know that during the war the business almost failed; a casualty which, unfortunately, resulted in the dismissal of my father's faithful employees. Although my brother's later success must have been based upon our mutual inheritance, I considered my share, to this date, had been used for Helena's education. This letter to me was not only a monstrous affront but filled me with suspicion as to the source of such wealth.

I wrote to my brother that without further investigation Helena should have no part in this inheritance and that I would make further enquiries through you.

No one save myself has given Helena the love I read in your eyes. You are Helena's future. In you lies the secret of her happiness. So it is to you I must turn for a decision I feel I no longer have the right to make for myself. Serious letters often make a fool of the writer. I willingly run this risk for the sake of Helena, knowing that neither you, nor she, will blame me in the happy event of my being proved wrong.

If the friend about whom I enquired of my brother is still in the city he will find the true source of Helena's inheritance. I suspect from my brother's anger that he still lives, and if he does, he is a man who will be easily located. Yet under these circumstances, you will agree, I cannot myself approach him.

So Thomas, I write to you this letter, which you will receive at the Embassy and not at your rooms where Helena might well be with you.

At present Helena is completely protected by ignorance of an inheritance and the suspicion I entertain. I would like to protect you too, Thomas, for you are young and you may feel that any part in such an investigation might endanger your career. So I will withhold the name of the man my brother fears until I hear from you. I will abide by your judgement, for Helena has chosen you and her happiness is based, I know, on her trust in your integrity.

This is a strange letter. You are an intelligent young man and will wonder how any woman can be moved enough to write like this unless it is impossible to find the words of the exact message she would like to convey. This is quite right. I cannot, and because of some obscure presentiment, dare not find the words.

However, twenty years away from a beloved city is long enough to acquire patience. Knowing Helena to be in Istanbul is, in a way, the same as being there myself. The city will give to her children the answer that love requires of them. Until that time, I await your reply.

From Helena

Mummy darling, you will have to be patient and let me start at the beginning. Please do not mind if I put in too much, otherwise I might omit something of importance, which I cannot afford to do. Just keep remembering that when I was a girl setting off to boarding school, you told me that if ever I found myself in an inextricable dilemma, to write down the facts, address them to you, seal the envelope and carry the letter around in my pocket. Nine times out of ten, you advised me, the writing down would clear the muddle and allow me to destroy the letter, while in the meantime nobody would open a letter to a girl's mother, even though there could be some who might stoop to peep into a diary. You know, of course, that having written I could never destroy, so sooner or later you always got the letter and thereby a large, if often redundant, share of my dilemma. You can expect the worst again. This time you are really in for a communication that I only hope will not be delivered to you as part of my personal effects.

Already I am confused enough to be living in another world where I cannot account for my actions. I might as well be a puppet, except I know I am being moved helplessly in a direction of which I subconsciously approve. Even so, I do not know where I am going or why I should be going there. In order to go, I have discovered in myself a capacity for lies and deceit. I have upset, without the slightest regret, Uncle Roger, who is fond of me and has been as kind as his nature allows. Thomas, whose condition is such that in no circumstances should I cause him anxiety, has forbidden me to go. Most important of all, but last on my list, so has the law!

So I must begin at the beginning, which was the very night of my arrival in Istanbul, when Thomas and I were having dinner together in a small restaurant where he hoped we would have complete privacy, even though we were dining in public. Try as I will, I cannot remember whether Thomas, at the time of his startling remark, was philosophising, making love, or combining both just to be teasingly facetious, because we were both so happy to be together again.

'Take a certain given point of light,' Thomas said. 'Your eye is attracted to it, hovers around it no more than a second, and yet sometimes, darling, from that single point your mind flashes out like the rays of the sun in a hundred directions.' There may have been a pause before he continued, 'Your eyes – Helena, what are you looking at?'

For it was in this moment that for the first time since our arrival my eyes left Thomas and fell upon a point of light that was the forehead of a man. This man's brow shone above a face so strongly carved that the skin was stretched over the structure like thin brown wrapping paper.

'Thomas,' I whispered, 'There is one of your points of light on the forehead of a man sitting at the corner table beyond your right shoulder. You are quite right about the flash of the mind. I have seen the man's face before but I don't know where or how. He is not young, Thomas; he is wearing a turban but is strangely beardless. His face looks naked somehow under the turban. He is wearing a robe but he doesn't appear to be the Arab his dress suggests. He is not looking at me but I cannot help looking at him. He has a remarkable face, even from this distance.'

Thomas smiled and leaned his head right up against mine so he could whisper back. 'Whatever you do, don't stare. He always sits there. His name is Rupert Augustinian.'

'You are joking. Rupert of Henzau in disguise, perhaps, but not a Roman emperor and Armenian too in Arab clothing.'

'Armenian darling, with a Scots mother, I'm told.'

'What is he – a secret agent?'

'If you want to be romantic – perhaps.'

'Is he or isn't he, Thomas?'

'It could be one of those things he is or has been from what people say.'

'How exciting. Do you know him?'

'Everybody knows him. He's a landmark. Every night he sits in that corner, dressed as he is now, waiting.'

'What for? Have you heard what for?'

'His wife.'

I pulled my head back. 'Really, Thomas, you are impossible.'

'You will see,' said Thomas smugly. 'She will come. She always does. She stays an hour or so and then he takes her upstairs.'

'Upstairs?'

'They live upstairs.'

'You are too provocative, Thomas, and I might add, too credible. I don't believe you, so there.'

'You will,' Thomas said. 'If you like this place and want to come here again, time will prove me right.'

'So far,' I told Thomas, 'I find this place fascinating. In fact, you may well end up being sick of the place yourself by too close acquaintance with it if you refuse to tell me the history of that man's face.'

'Is man not a unity then, darling? Can his face have a separate history?'

'It's no use trying to put me off. I have seen the face before and I'll find out.'

'You have not been in Istanbul before, my darling Helena, unless you are hiding your past from me.'

One of those moments happened then. Thomas did put me off just by catching my eyes and I don't know how long it was before he said, 'Your hair is so lovely, Helena. Let's get out of here.' He beckoned to the waiter and ordered our coffee.

Some time during dinner I'd noticed the waiter wasn't particularly affable and didn't smile, yet seemed somehow without either arrogance or servility. He gave the impression that service of food was necessary to sustain life but that life is a serious business in Istanbul. Is that Turkish?

The restaurant, though not large, was filled to capacity. The food was good enough and the coffee excellent, but after one puff of Thomas' Turkish cigarette I nearly choked. I glanced again at Rupert Augustinian and was startled to see him look in our direction before he rose and reached out an incredibly long arm to pull out the chair that faced him. He stood for a minute, very straight, and must have been fully four inches above six feet in height – an unusually imposing figure. When he moved he swayed stiffly rather than walked to the door that opened behind him.

The woman he met at the door and helped into the chair was very small and slightly bent. Her dress, shoes and stockings were black but the shawl she wore over her shoulders was magnificently embroidered with red and gold silk thread. When she was carefully established he re-seated himself abruptly yet with deliberation. There was an air of fragility about the small figure of the woman that had that bird-like quality, as if without feathers there would be no more than the intricacy of tiny brittle bones.

'The lady has just arrived,' I informed Thomas.

'Don't stare, darling,' Thomas whispered urgently. 'Stop staring. He doesn't like it when she is there'.

'I don't blame him,' I answered softly. 'Anyway, he's not looking this way, as it happens. Just the same, you'd think they'd be used to staring after twenty years.'

'Even after twenty years I'll resent people staring too long at you, my sweet. In his case they say he's apt to throw starers out on their necks. Shall we go now?'

We rose, and putting on my wrap gave Thomas a chance to touch my hair. I can never get over how much Thomas loves my hair. Really, I can't. I suppose we were obviously very much in love because as we started to go out a strange thing happened. Rupert Augustinian put out his long arm as we passed his table and touched Thomas on the coat sleeve. 'So she has come,' he said to Thomas in a soft, deep English that made the whole sentence he spoke sound like one word.

'Yes, Mr Augustinian,' Thomas said proudly. 'She has come. My fiancée just arrived in Istanbul today. Helena, may I present Mr and Mrs Augustinian.'

The tiny lady in black nodded her head in a strange way and whispered, '*Si. Si.*'

She's Spanish, I thought, but of course, naturally. Thomas had told me this restaurant was in Galata, the home of the Spanish Jews. I didn't look down at her face. I was looking up at Augustinian, who had risen and was addressing himself to Thomas. A queer sensation flowed through me again, with such force that I was left quite speechless, scarcely able to smile. The man's eyes, black as hawks and equally hidden under wrinkled eyelids, flashed but momentarily into my own before he finished speaking to Thomas.

'Tonight the moon will not show you her face; but tomorrow night go to Ayub.' He didn't smile as he spoke. Dismissed as suddenly as we were summoned, we moved hand-in-hand into the street.

'Why ever did he say to go to – to where was it, Thomas?'

'Ayub. When the moon is bright it's one of the loveliest places in Istanbul for lovers. It's the place where Pierre Loti sat writing his poetry, looking down at the Golden Horn.'

'Whoever would have thought a Turk could be so romantic? They seem to look so serious all the time, especially that face of Augustinian's, with his fierce eyes.'

'My little darling,' Thomas said, so protectively tucking my arm in his. 'Be obsessed with my face, not the face of Augustinian. We've only another hour and then I must take you back to your uncle.'

'Whatever do you have to do tonight, Thomas, that is so important I can't come too?'

'Merely the work of an unimportant third secretary meeting a plane for a bag of mail. Wilton is a bit of a stickler for protocol and if I take you, my darling, I might jeopardise my chances of getting a promotion through in time to make you the wife of a second secretary. Now do you understand?'

'I understand I'm going to marry the nicest and most promising young man in the service.'

'The luckiest, you mean,' Thomas said.

You must excuse me for that. I had to put it in out of sheer vanity. I still can't believe it's true about Thomas and me. I know you understand and won't hold it against me if I leave out the rest of the conversation. Believe me, it wasn't long enough before Thomas took me back to Uncle Roger's house. You told me about the house, but do you know, I wouldn't have recognised it at all from your description. Uncle Roger, I think, must be far richer than we ever thought, for he must have spent a fortune on this house.

My room on the second floor is the guest room of a princess. Pale blue satin-studded walls, cream and gold chairs, and a mirage of mirrors on a rose carpet, inches thick. At first, when I was dressing to go out to dinner with Thomas I felt rather like a giraffe in a hot-house, all legs and arms and neck. So, you will know what I mean when I tell you that after dinner with Thomas, I lay in the centre of the huge, glamorous bed like a little girl in fairyland, overawed with love and wonder, gloating for the thousandth time over my meeting with Thomas in London at Uncle Roger's hotel.

'Oh Thomas, meet my niece, Helena. As a matter of fact, she will be going to Cypress about the same time you return to Istanbul.'

'Hello Helena.'

'Hello Thomas.'

Sizing each other up, outwardly nonchalant while our heads were turning upside down. Making keep-your-distance conversation under the eyes of Uncle Roger.

And then Thomas and Helena together at lunch in the West-end.

Dinner in Soho.

Tea at Lyons Corner House.

Sandwiches in Hyde Park before staring in shop windows.

Thomas and Helena engaged, trying to extend Thomas's leave.

Helena in tears waving farewell.

Thomas miraculously in Cypress to meet her boat. Uncle Roger's note: 'Why not visit Istanbul? Your mother can spare you. You can shop here, not to mention seeing Thomas in person, to plan your wedding before his transfer next April.'

Me, the Helena of all this, unable to sleep in the unaccustomed luxury of the bed, twisting Thomas's ring on my finger, switching on the shell-pink lamp to study his photograph, encouraging sleep, to dream about him, and only succeeding in a wide-awake recollection of every minute of the day from Uncle Roger's first greeting. 'Thomas is looking after you for dinner. I'll be out late, previous arrangement, that's how business is here,' to the last word of the strange man Rupert Augustinian, which left Thomas and me, two lovers alone, again planning our wonderful hours together in the golden city.

First thing in the morning Thomas was going to phone me, before I got up and he went to work. His voice would be the first I would hear on the new day.

But there was no ring on the gold and white telephone. I was awakened by the hand of Uncle Roger shaking my shoulder and Uncle Roger's voice assailing my ears.

'Helena, wake up. Helena, Helena.'

'Hello Uncle Roger.' I stretched my arms wide, remembered where I was and sprang up in joy, only to sit back again for there was an odd restraint about Uncle Roger's presence that struck sudden terror to my heart.

'Thomas?' I whispered.

'Listen to me, Helena.' Uncle Roger was brusque. 'There is no worst. Just a strange occurrence. Do you hear me?'

'Uncle Roger, what is it? Tell me what it is.'

'There's an embassy official waiting downstairs to see you. He wants to ask you a few questions. Your sane answers will help. It seems that Thomas collected the diplomatic bag last night and then disappeared.'

'Disappeared – Uncle Roger!'

'As far as we know there were no valuables in the bag, no money or securities, no accident has been reported.'

'Thomas has disappeared – Thomas! Oh, Uncle Roger!'

Uncle Roger was shockingly severe. His voice was just like ice. 'If you must cry, Helena, please get it over with. Thomas has disappeared and must be found. The sooner you can dress and see Mr Wilton the quicker the authorities can get on with finding him. You spent last evening with Thomas. You saw him last.'

'I'll dress now, Uncle Roger,' I said, stung awake – which I expect was exactly what he intended. 'You needn't worry, I won't cry.'

'I had coffee brought up for you,' Uncle Roger said.

'I don't need it.'

'Yes, you do. Drink, Helena. I'll pour it while you dress.'

There were two cups on the tray. Uncle Roger poured a black cup for himself, took it into the hall and waited.

There were three men waiting to see me in Uncle Roger's library, Mr Wilton from the Embassy, another Embassy official called Ferguson who spoke like a London policeman and a uniformed member of the Turkish police force.

'Your uncle has given us the details of your arrival,' the man, Ferguson, said. 'We are only interested in the time you spent alone with your fiancé after you left here last night.'

'I'll try to remember,' I said.

'Do sit down, my dear,' Mr Wilton interjected. 'Sit here on the couch, or yes, that will be all right. Now, Ferguson.'

I sat on a chair opposite Uncle's desk and tried to tell them where Thomas had taken me around Istanbul before dinner when he was showing me in advance the places we were going to explore together, pointing out I remembered Aya Sofya, the Seraglio, Santa Irene and the covered market.

'You went to all those places by taxi, Miss Martine?'

'It wasn't very long, really,' I said. 'Only long enough to show me a little of the city before we had dinner.'

'Can you remember where you dined?' Mr Wilton asked. I understood then that I must have been incoherent about the first part of our evening. For a moment I wavered between anger and tears. Was I to tell these men that I had been looking at Thomas more than the sights of Istanbul? That I had known I was to see everything again? That Thomas and I were riding around in a taxi only to be alone with each other?

Into the silence the man Ferguson said sharply, 'It would help if you could remember something about the place where you dined, Miss Martine.'

'I know exactly where I dined!' I said, astounded to hear my voice rising in a shrill crescendo. 'We dined in the Spanish suburb near the docks, at a little place Thomas knew.'

'Do you remember the name, Miss Martine?'

'Yes, I do. The restaurant is owned by a man called Rupert Augustinian.'

A rifle shot could not have startled the four men more than that name. Uncle Roger moved suddenly from where he was standing beside me and almost collapsed in the chair behind his desk. As I looked towards him my eyes fell on a huge oil painting of a Spanish dancer that hung on the wall directly behind the desk in an elaborate gilt frame. This may surprise you, but I was startled because it was the only old thing I had seen so far in the whole house.

'Was your fiancé – did your fiancé seem – familiar with Augustinian?' Mr Wilton asked. He has a very quiet voice and I found his questions easier to answer.

'He had been several times before. I know that because he told me a little about the Turkish friend who introduced him to the Augustinians. They often dine together there.'

'Do you know the Turkish friend's name, Miss Martine?'

'I can't remember his name, but I am to meet him at an Embassy party, Thomas said. He works with Thomas.'

'I know the man she means,' Mr Wilton said. 'Thank you very much, Miss Martine.' He wrote something down in his book. But it didn't mean they were finished with me.

Ferguson said, 'Did your fiancé have any conversation with anybody but yourself in that restaurant?'

Something about the way he said it frightened me more than even the fact that Thomas was lost. His voice threatened Thomas. I glanced at my uncle imploringly.

'Try to answer the question, Helena,' Uncle Roger replied sternly.

'He only talked to the waiter to order the food. He didn't know the waiter if that's what you mean. The waiter didn't seem to treat us any different to anyone else who was there. He was very busy. There were no empty tables while we dined.'

'I see. And nobody else spoke to you?'

'Only the proprietor as we went out.'

I felt every man stiffen again.

'What did the proprietor say, Miss Martine?'

The sudden clear recollection of Rupert Augustinian and what he had said to Thomas startled my intuitive brain wide awake. He had said, 'So she has come.' He had meant me, but these men might think he had meant something in the diplomatic bag. This would make Thomas some sort of accessory instead of the victim I knew that he was. A slur on Thomas's reputation would interfere with his promotion. Thomas wanted so much to make me the wife of a second secretary.

'The proprietor only wished us goodnight,' I said.

'In what way did he wish you goodnight, Miss Martine?' Mr Wilton asked gently. 'Did he speak English to you?'

'Yes, I didn't understand at first – his words all ran together.'

'Then he didn't actually say the words goodnight.'

'No, he made a remark about the moon.'

'Miss Martine, in view of the seriousness of this situation, I must tell you I believe you are withholding something.'

'Mr Ferguson,' Uncle said sharply.

Mr Wilton spoke again to me, ignoring both Uncle Roger and Ferguson. 'Do you remember, Miss Martine?'

I looked down. 'We were a longish time over dinner, Mr Wilton. I suppose everybody was watching us. I – I hadn't seen my fiancé for so long. The proprietor made a joke as we went out. What he said was it was too bad there was no moon.'

Mr Wilton relaxed, but Uncle and Mr Ferguson did not. 'I see,' he said.

'Mr Wilton,' I burst out, 'Why are you asking me all these questions? Where is Thomas? What do you think has happened to him? Haven't you any idea what has happened to him? What am I going to do?'

'You are going to do nothing at all for the time being. I am going to have to ask you to carry on as if nothing has happened. It is essential that nothing is known about this matter, that it goes no further than your-self and your uncle. We will keep you informed of all developments. If you will excuse us now.'

The three men filed out of the room under Uncle Roger's escort. I was left alone facing the oil painting of the Spanish dancer.

Torn between fear for Thomas himself and a new but even greater fear for his reputation, I had started my second full day in Istanbul by lying to the law. Or had I lied? Do you lie when you refrain from hand-ing over for public consumption, remarks which may have a significance you have not yet understood yourself? To avoid giving way to panic and tears, I concentrated as hard as I could on the two remarks of the man Rupert Augustinian.

'So she has come.' I was expected and 'The moon will not show her face tonight. But tomorrow night go to Ayub.'

In spite of my effort, panic rose up inside of me. Three short sen-tences from a man called Rupert Augustinian. The first sentence was true. I was not still dreaming about it or imagining it. I really was in Is-tanbul. The second sentence was true. The moon had not shown her face, neither her own nor mine last night. And the third sentence was an instruction that had not yet come to pass. If the third sentence was true then I should go to Ayub and there, it seemed to me, I would find some connection with Thomas. But why? And what if all the sentences were true in some other sense? And why was the face of the man Au-gustinian so familiar? Where had I seen his likeness before? Thomas had laughed at me over that, but there had been no deception in Thomas. I must hang on to that, I told myself. There was no deception in Thomas.

Belligerently, I stared at the Spanish dancer, focusing upon her my belief in Thomas. It was strange but my spirit absorbed defiance from the attitude of her posture. There is something about Spanish dancing, some rare quality of justifiable fury that stamps upon a world that so cruelly tosses human beings into constant dilemma.

'I believe in Thomas,' I silently informed the portrait. 'I know there is no deception in Thomas. So Thomas just has to be found. You can just give me an idea that will help me, you with your beautifully controlled body, your proud head and your exquisite fluttering hands.'

Such was the passion of my faith in Thomas, I trembled. The portrait of the Spanish dancer trembled with me, as if life were flowing into her again after all the years she had hung up on that wall. Some artist had captured her image when she was in her prime, but years fell upon her as I gazed with angry, defiant eyes and she seemed to shrink; her little hands contracted. Astonished, I knew without a doubt that the Spanish dancer was a portrait of the wife of Rupert Augustinian.

From the door of the library, Uncle Roger spoke to me. 'Are you stuck to that chair, Helena?' he asked with attempted levity. 'I'm hungry. Come and join me for breakfast.'

I rose and followed him, and without appetite attempted to eat. When the butler left us with our second cups of coffee, Uncle Roger made another effort to cheer me. He didn't mean to make me resentful, but of course as usual, I had to be. He has an unfortunate way of saying things. 'Well, Helena,' Uncle Roger said, 'You have considerably more stamina than I expected. Your mother would be washed away in tears by now.' He was trying to be kind, paying be a compliment in his own way, but I was miserable.

'I'm, terribly worried, Uncle Roger.'

'I know, my dear,' he said. 'Believe me, so am I.'

'Why were you all so upset when I said Thomas and I dined at Augustinian's?'

'Because you muddled up everything else and then remembered his name perfectly. Augustinian is notorious. Why in God's name Thomas had to take you there the night of your arrival I'll never know. The boy must be mad.'

'Thomas said everybody goes there. What is Mr Augustinian notorious for?'

'Himself. His name is connected with all kinds of rackets in the city. He's too clever to be caught, of course – just sits there. But he knows everything. Why didn't you tell them what he really said to you?'

'I did the best I could.'

'Augustinian never cracked a joke about the moon in his life, Helena. He doesn't crack jokes. He's too big.'

I couldn't tell whether Uncle Roger meant actual physical size or something more sinister.

'Then perhaps he really meant what he said?' I remarked tentatively.

'Which was?' Uncle Roger asked quickly.

'That Thomas should take me to see Ayub tonight when the moon is up, seeing last night was so cloudy. Uncle Roger, will you take me to Ayub tonight to find Thomas?'

Uncle Roger absolutely bristled. 'Take you to Ayub at Augustinian's suggestion? I certainly will not. I am not a boy like Thomas, Helena. I happen to be worth a great deal of money and you are my niece. This business of Thomas is quite enough. We will not go near Ayub on the suggestion of Rupert Augustinian.'

'Then I must go alone, Uncle Roger, to find Thomas.'

'You will not go to find Thomas. Ayub is the last place to find Thomas, the one place in which you would have no hope of finding Thomas. Anything could happen to you at Ayub. It is that kind of place.'

I said, with sudden unexpected vanity, 'I could hide my hair, Uncle Roger.'

Poor Uncle Roger, he was under considerable strain as it was. He produced a wry little grimace that only got as far as his upper lip. 'I presume you wore your hair as it is now, last night?' he said.

'Yes, I did. Thomas loves it this way.'

'He would. Pity you didn't have it done up under a little hat as it was when you arrived. You looked exceptionally smart, I thought.'

'Why is it a pity?' I asked, ruffled.

'Because the women of our family have always been proud of their hair. I suppose you'll keep yours the same colour as your mother's until you are as old as she is!'

I pulled in my lips and reminded myself that even as an invited guest and a relative I was none the less already a trial in this regulated, bachelor household. Besides, maybe I do look like you a little after all, because you were definitely on Uncle Roger's mind and I think this annoyed him in some perverse way that morning.

'Your mother was a beauty,' he continued snappily, 'But that was not the reason other people had to go around picking up the debris. When you came up from school in London, it did not strike me that you had the same quality.'

You can imagine how I felt. I was furious, as I had a right to be, but a bit flattered too, darling, if you will forgive me for telling you this about Uncle Roger. You did warn me he might not be nice about you. Just the same, I couldn't let the remark pass.

'Thank you,' I said acidly, 'but it happens I'm too tall, too bony, too practical and too frank to be like Mother. I have nothing but the hair.'

'The quality I speak of overrides appearance, except of course, you have her eyes.' He paused and then added, 'We all have fine eyes. I should have realised also, Helena, that the small, cuddly type of women idolised by my generation has been overtaken by tall, thin young women who show their bones.'

As you can imagine, I was flabbergasted, but I did not go through school as the Anne of Green Gables type, carrots and all, for nothing. Knowing, unfortunately, that my height when I stood exceeded his own, I eyed Uncle Roger severely across the table.

'You may think that, Uncle Roger,' I said, 'but you are wrong. It is because I am tall and bony that I must find Thomas, who is much taller and much bonier than I am and therefore is the only man I have found who suits me. He loves me and I love him, and even if you are sorry you asked me here to stay, I won't go back to Cypress until he is found. So you might as well take me to Ayub if there is a chance he is there.'

Something in Uncle Roger shrank and I found myself feeling sorry for him. After all, Thomas's disappearance was not his fault.

'Thomas won't be found at Ayub,' he said, 'besides, I had arranged a small dinner party tonight to introduce you and Thomas to some of my associates.'

'Oh, Uncle Roger, that was kind of you. Whatever can we do?'

'Do? I will cancel it, of course. You without Thomas is impossible. You heard Wilton, didn't you? I will say you and Thomas lunched rashly and are impossibly ill. For the sake of my servants you will remain in your room.'

'While you take me to Ayub to find Thomas.'

Almost a miracle happened then. Uncle Roger looked defeated, as if he had been through the same ordeal many times in other circumstances and couldn't be bothered arguing further. Or else he felt he just had to get me out of his sight. 'I will not take you to Ayub,' he said, but then he asked, 'Did you notice my chauffeur when we met you at the airport?'

'No, Uncle Roger.'

'I didn't think you did. That's the advantage the tall and bony types like Thomas have over other men. Well, to continue, Joe, his real name is Joe Osman, has been my chauffeur for several years. He's the oldest staff I have on here. I'll send you out with him in the car this afternoon and he will drive you near enough to show you that Thomas will not be found at Ayub. You will not leave the car. Then he will bring you home so you can retire to bed well before the estimated time of the dinner party.' He stood up as he was speaking. 'Come along,' he added, 'I'll ring for Joe in the library.'

There is another thing that being tall and bony teaches you and that is to take the most you can get without sticking out for more. I shut my mouth tight and followed Uncle Roger into the library. Once there, I sat down in the same chair as before and fixed my eye again on the Spanish dancer.

Uncle Roger rang for the chauffeur. To make conversation while we were waiting, I said amiably, 'She's lovely.'

'What?'

'She's lovely,' I repeated, 'The Spanish dancer behind you.'

'I know where the picture is,' Uncle Roger snapped, then he recovered himself and was amiable too. 'Good oil, isn't it?'

'The artist must have been very good to get her so exactly.'

'What's that?'

'I mean you can tell it's a portrait not an imaginary Spanish dancer. You can almost feel her dancing.'

'Strange you should say that.'

'Why?'

He hesitated. 'Because I think you are right.'

'Did you know her, Uncle Roger – the dancer, I mean?'

'Yes, I knew her, years ago. She was a girlfriend of mine.'

I could have strangled the chauffeur, Joe Osman, who knocked on the door at that moment.

'Joe,' Uncle Roger said. 'After lunch I want you to take my niece shopping. She wants to buy brocade for her trousseau. After she chooses, have the stuff and the account sent to me. If there's any time left, run her up to Ayub for a view of the Horn. I want her to see as much of the city as we can arrange while she is here and I can't spare you every day. She must be back here before dark, to rest before the guests arrive.'

Whereupon Joe Osman made a rapid speech to Uncle in Turkish and Uncle made an equally rapid reply in the same language, before he said to me abruptly, 'Be ready at one, Helena. And put your smartest hat on. We'll start together. Joe can drop me off.'

Joe Osman, a taciturn middle-aged man with enormous, almost luminous eyes in a dark face, remained standing stolidly like part of the furniture, to the right of the door. Obviously he was not the one expected to leave and I was.

'I'll be ready, Uncle,' I said, 'and thanks for the brocade.'

'Be sure you know what you want and how much of it, Joe will do the rest for you. Shopping is one of his specialties,' Uncle Roger replied and dismissed me.

I passed close to Joe Osman as I went out the door. He was looking at me and through me at the same time, like a man memorising the page of a book. I looked straight at him and nodded, not bothering to smile. A smile was somehow superfluous.

You would have been amused to see me looking over my wardrobe, in order to be suitably dressed for such a promising afternoon. It was not clear in just which direction the promise lay, except that I had won my way to Ayub, so I was nervous as a cat, unable to concentrate on a book, honourably debarred from writing to you, with plenty of time on my hands. The wall of mirrors kept reflecting my hair as I prowled restlessly from one side of the room to the other. Hiding my hair obviously had to be a first consideration. I decided to wear the glamorous blue turban affair I bought in the first mad moment of my engagement, when I had hopes of one day being sophisticated enough as a young matron to wear it. It seems at my present rate of progress I may never become the sophisticated matron, but I have had my money's worth out of the hat, which covered every hair on my head with Mata Hari thoroughness. The only dress of the daytime variety that matched the headpiece was the straight blue linen, which is supposed to have line. With my hair out of sight, this garment emphasised every protruding bone in my neck and reminded me, for the sake of my vanity, of a nice long, cold glass of water. Finally, without touching the tray of lunch delivered at noon, I completed my disguise with an extravagant amount of eye make-up and a heavily outlined lipstick. Then, after controlling my agitation for another thirty elongated minutes, I went downstairs at exactly one o'clock.

Uncle Roger was not alone but enjoying coffee with two Turkish associates, father and son. After prolonged pleasantries, during which the son flattered me by a most consistent stare and Uncle ignored me almost completely, we were driven to Istanbul in the associate's car by Joe Osman, with his chauffeur's hat between himself and the owner of the car on the front seat. During the drive from Beyoglu nobody took the trouble to point out to me the landmarks of this remarkable city, but I knew we were in old Istanbul after I recognised the Galata Bridge and the wonderful skyline of mosques and minarets over the other side of the water. Uncle Roger carried on a jerky conversation with his friend in the front seat. The young man continued to flatter me with the look of a sailor who has not seen a woman for six dreary months at sea. When we eventually pulled up in a narrow street of musty shops, I had begun to wonder if the hat was going to be the success I had hoped for.

In front of the brocade bazaar a shuffle took place. Joe Osman got out with his hat in his hand. The elderly gentleman moved into the driver's seat. Uncle moved in beside him and the solicitous young man, having raced around from his side of the car to the street to help me out, appeared unwilling to get back in again. Uncle said something curt to him in Turkish that made him blush and made me feel simply ridiculous. Then the young man got in and the car drove off. Joe Osman piloted me through a door into a kind of harem made of silk brocades where I felt almost sick with anticipation and atrociously conspicuous. The brocades were fabulous, yet I was so painfully nervous about getting to Ayub I chose a silk that Joe Osman would not let me buy. He was politely considerate but determined I should have the quality of a magnificent sea-green brocade of his selection. So much for my escape from green into a blue turban! I accepted his judgement, but added a length of silvered white that looked more than expensive enough to meet with his approval. During the bargaining to adjust the price, I waited tensely near the door until eventually Joe Osman accompanied me out into the street.

'Now,' he said, 'we go to the covered market.'

'No, to Ayub, please.'

'But first the covered market for your choice. It is but twenty minutes to Ayub.'

'I would like to see Ayub now, please. There is not much time to be back before dark.'

His strange eyes glowed but he did not argue. 'The car is this way, Miss.'

In the first side street beyond the bazaar he opened for me the door of the car in which I had driven from the airport to Uncle Roger's house. When I was comfortably established in the back seat he put on his chauffeur's hat and drove slowly forward in the narrow street. As we turned the first corner I sat up in amazement to see a man with a piano on his back.

'Galata Jews,' Joe Osman said, in answer to my shocked query. 'Strong as horses, have lived in Galata since their forefathers came as refugees from the Spanish inquisition.'

'But how can they carry such loads? It's incredible.'

'For them it is a secret from the father to the son.'

'Surely carrying such weight shortens their lives?'

'They sit in the streets, one hundred years old,' Joe said.

I decided then to address Joe as Mr Osman for I recognised in him a man to be respected and 'Joe' to me was not respect. I asked him if Istanbul was his home town.

'I was born in Idirna,' he said, 'but have lived here many years, for here in the city lived the father of my mother.'

'Did you come from Idirna by boat?' I asked. To this question I received an unexpected reply that put a satisfactory end to further discussion on a personal level. 'I do not know how I came,' he said. 'It is enough that I arrived as my mother wished, to the house of her father.'

There was one thing I knew I must not do. In no way should I allow Joe Osman to think that I considered this trip in any other light than that of an interested tourist.

'Are all the houses in Istanbul made of wood?' I asked.

'Nearly all wood,' he replied, as if that disposed of houses.

'Those trellised buildings look very old,' I persisted. 'They lean right over. I shouldn't think they would be safe to live in.'

He did not comment. So I went right ahead, undaunted, my voice deliberately bright with interest.

'And some of the wood looks splintered. I suppose it is because the people can't afford to paint them. Is it very expensive to paint a house?'

'It is not considered,' he said. 'We eat, that is all you understand. We eat and we have education.'

'And the most beautiful city in the world.'

'The city, she's always been rich, Miss, the people poor.'

I thought rather guiltily of Uncle's house, which most decidedly did not lack paint. We passed a great mosque beside a slender minaret and I wondered if it was here that Mustafa Kemal ordered the tarbrushes from the heads of the faithful.

'You must have very good schools in Istanbul,' I said. 'You speak wonderful English.'

'There are schools for all in the city who wish to learn.'

'Do you have children, Mr Osman?' It was out before I thought.

'No children,' he said and I could have bitten my tongue because it was quite evident that he was willing to speak as a guide, but not as a person.

'Tomorrow,' I said in desperation, 'I hope I will be able to come here to the Seraglio to see the treasures. My fiancé tells me there are gold cups studded with precious stones. It will be interesting to see them, but I'd hate to drink out of one. Imagine swallowing a ruby or a diamond by mistake.' I twisted the ring on my engagement finger.

'You will come many days, not one. There is a day for gold, a day for the armoury, another day for Aya Sofya, Santa Irene and the Mosques. Many days are needed for the walls and domes of the Scray.'

On safe ground at last, I questioned him about the ancient fortress above the waters of the Golden Horn, the old buildings I would see and the best time of day to go to Leander's Tower. A patient guide, he satisfied with facts and figures, avoiding critical judgements of his own as no concern of mine. I surmised he knew a great many things he did not say. He told me briefly the history of the last Ottoman Sultanate as if I were a small child; overlooking interruptions, waiting until I was able to frame questions. And all the time we were driving slowly towards Ayub, by a devious route perhaps, because it must have been more than half an hour before we came to a cemetery and the wonderful Mosque of Ayub above the Golden Horn. I think I was surprised when Osman almost stopped to point out the mosque as we drove past. I assumed then that he was accepting my curiosity in a natural way, and I was glad because I knew this was my only hope of getting out of the car. High above the waters, I saw the hill that must be the famous view and asked him to stop. I could sense his reluctance in the sudden stiffening of his shoulders.

'But Mr Osman,' I said. 'My uncle doesn't mind if we stop for a minute as long as I am back before dark.'

'You will come again, it is sure.'

'It is not sure. This is probably my only opportunity, my fiancé does not have a car. Besides, Mr Osman, I'm stiff. I would like to stretch my legs.'

'Here?' he said. 'It is not yet the view.'

'Why not here?' I said desperately. 'This is Ayub isn't it? Here will do as well as anywhere else.'

He did not answer but slowed the car to a stop a little off the road facing the turn. When he opened the car door, I stepped out. The air was very still and it was unbelievably beautiful in that place. Overcome by the sudden pulse of my emotions, I stood for a moment and breathed in the sea air before I began to climb a path among the cypress trees that graced the hill. Joe Osman walked close behind me but he did not speak. I think I was glad of his silent presence because the atmosphere of this place passed beyond beauty into an eerie presentiment. I had no conscious knowledge of this place and yet it stirred in me a recognition.

I stopped just before the path turned and smiled disarmingly at Osman, who had drawn suddenly abreast, swung round and faced me, his eyes glancing back at the car. Still neither of us spoke, yet I knew I could go no further. Osman did not even smile but I think it was a kind of concession that he put his hand into his pocket and pulled out a crumpled packet of cigarettes. As he bent his head to shelter the match in his two hands, I looked past him, further up the hill.

A little distance away a man was sitting on a seat under an ancient cypress. Discovering him there was to admit a ghost; an apparition. For the fraction of a second my head swam to the thumping of my heart. Then

I darted past Osman, who was the only obstacle between myself and the wooden seat. Osman's hand shot out to stop me but I was too quick and running like a deer, so that I was only dimly conscious of the sudden halt of Osman's feet as he pounded the road running behind me. Too breathless to speak, I arrived at the side of Rupert Augustinian.

'Mr Augustinian,' I gasped.

He turned and regarded me with the initial surprise of a man contemplating an aggravating child.

'Good afternoon,' he said and I knew he recognised me, in spite of the make-up and hat. 'You are too early for the moon,' he added and his deep voice sounded hard and uncompromising.

'Mr Augustinian,' I said. 'Where is Thomas? I shouldn't be here. I will have to go – any minute I will have to go. Where is Thomas?'

'Thomas?' Mr Augustinian said.

'My fiancé, Thomas Pringle, who I was with last night in your restaurant.'

'Are you frightened?' Rupert Augustinian said then, as if he were making a statement rather than asking a question.

'Frightened! Mr Augustinian, I have run away from my uncle's chauffeur to speak to you. I'm desperate. I must find Thomas. Please, tell me where he is.'

Quite suddenly then my face puckered in an excruciating effort to hold back a deluge of tears. What had I expected of this man? Who was he? Why did I think he would help me? I turned my face from him.

'Don't let them come – the tears,' he said. 'They help nothing. Sit down. Get your breath and begin at the beginning.'

'You said to come here. You said so to Thomas.' My voice was very nearly a sob. I bit my lip hard.

'Begin at the beginning!' It was a command if softly spoken, inexplicably compelling.

I choked.

'Then I will begin. What frightened you? Was it the man running after you?'

'That was only Mr Osman, the chauffeur.'

Could I have imagined he laughed? A sense of unreality enveloped me. Where was Joe Osman? Why hadn't he come? Alarmed, I looked around me.

'What are you frightened of?' Mr Augustinian repeated.

'Thomas,' I whispered. 'Thomas is gone. I don't know where he is.'

'He was to meet you here, and he has not come, or he was with you here and he has disappeared?'

'It was last night he disappeared. He went to get the diplomatic bag from the airport and then he disappeared.'

'You have not been long in Istanbul, Miss – Helena he called you, did he not?'

'Yes. Helena Martine. I've been here two days. Mr Augustinian, do you know where Thomas is? Could you tell me he is all right?'

'I? You astound me. You have run from your uncle's chauffeur to me because you believe I know where your fiancé is?'

'Last night you said to come here. I heard you.'

'My dear young lady, you and your young man were interesting to me. I said to my wife, there are two children in love. The girl has red hair. There is an old proverb, "So she has come." It simply means the loved one – that a man has found his love. It is that which I said to your young man. Because I had told my wife you were there and in love and it is my habit to tell my wife such things. That is all.'

'But Thomas addressed you by name. He knew you.'

'Everybody knows me who dines in my restaurant. I am there every evening.'

'Then why are you here now?'

'I will be in my usual place at the usual hour.'

'But why are you here now? Why, just when I came, just when I knew you would be here?'

'You knew I would be here?'

'That's why I came. That's why I had to come. It was terribly difficult to come. The police think I am at home.'

'The police have told you to stay at home?'

'They are trying to find Thomas. Can't you understand, Mr Augustinian, don't you see? Anything could have happened to Thomas.'

'Did the police know that you dined at my tables last night?'

'Yes.'

'Does your uncle know that too?'

'Yes.'

'You came here to look for me despite all this?'

'Mr Augustinian, you must understand. I didn't tell them exactly what you said. I was trying to save Thomas. I know Thomas couldn't be mixed up in any—' I stopped. I was talking too easily to Rupert Augustinian.

'But I could be. You have been told that. You have learned many things very fast, have you not?'

'I have learned nothing at all,' I said sanely, to my own astonishment, as if suddenly I were years older and utterly resigned.

'Your young man is in the British Embassy.'

'How do you know that if you do not know him?'

'Do not be a foolish bird. You told me he disappeared with the diplomatic bag and that he is, shall we say, above reproach. Then how otherwise would he collect the bag that has disappeared with him? It appears the bag was golden.'

'The police said the bag contained only letters.'

'A particular kind of gold,' he said, in a voice so speculative it made me irritable.

'I do not care a fig about the bag. I am worried sick about Thomas.'

'The secret of the whereabouts of Thomas can only be known by the whereabouts of this bag.'

'Then you do not know where Thomas is.' It was a statement I made.

'I have told you, I do not know.'

'But you do know what has happened to my uncle's chauffeur, you must.' I sprang to my feet and faced him, terrified, yet not, strangely enough, of Rupert Augustinian himself, only of the place, because of

Osman, because of Thomas. 'What am I going to do? How will I get back?'

'Osman has merely been detained. He has been persuaded to wait until I have finished talking to you.'

'Who has detained him?'

'You ask many questions, Miss Helena. It is understandable. If you are ready to go back, you will find Osman in the car. I will return to Galata. My wife will still be waiting.'

'I don't want to go,' I said miserably. 'I don't want to go without Thomas. Would you want to go without your wife?' I flung at him then. 'Would you?'

'It is strange you do not trust the police.'

'Would you – in Istanbul?' I countered bitterly.

'A young woman should have faith in the institution of the law. You must have patience and wait.'

'I can't wait. Now that I have run away from Joe Osman my uncle will want to send me back to Cyprus. Thomas is my whole life and I won't go. Do you understand that? I won't go.'

'Do you not have parents who could come to wait with you until the police find Thomas?'

'My mother cannot come to Istanbul, I would not ask her. Peter has been sick and there are the boys to look after.'

'Peter?'

'My stepfather. It wouldn't help to worry him. He would feel useless and inadequate and that would not be fair.'

Rupert Augustinian rose to his feet. 'Very well, Helena,' he said. 'Would you like me to tell your uncle to keep you here, if he wants to send you home?'

I could scarcely believe I had heard him correctly. 'You know my uncle as well as that?'

'I know him, shall we say, as well as that.'

'Mr Augustinian, please, please help me find Thomas.'

'I will consider.'

'I beg you, Mr Augustinian. Your wife would want you to, I'm sure she would. She would have seen last night how much we love each other, Thomas and I.'

'My wife is blind.' Rupert Augustinian said, and turning from me abruptly began to walk ahead of me down the hill with the controlled, deliberate action of a man of steel. I walked very humbly behind him. Trust, even when you have forfeited all right to it, has a peculiar tenacity.

Uncle's car was standing where I had left it, and to my amazement Joe Osman was sitting behind the wheel, looking down at the Golden Horn, his face a mask set in stone, his eyes looking straight ahead. He did not turn his head when we drew abreast and Rupert Augustinian spoke. 'It is wiser, Osman, to omit this hour from the day.'

Osman nodded briefly. Mr Augustinian opened the back door of the car. 'Go back,' he said to me. 'Worry is useless. Sleep. But first, study your face. You do not do well to hide your hair. Without your hair the bone structure of your face is accentuated. Wait for five days. If you really need me, send Osman.'

I had no time to reply. Immediately, he shut the door and raised his hand. The car rolled forward.

My face was streaked with a mixture of heavy mascara and tears. I wiped it clean with my handkerchief. Then I pulled off my hat and combed my hair.

'What happened to you?' I demanded then of the Turk, Osman.

He did not reply.

'What are you going to tell my uncle?'

'You have heard,' he replied. 'When Rupert Augustinian says to forget an hour of a day, it is forgotten.'

'I do not know what happened to you.'

'When he says sleep – sleep,' Osman replied.

The house was very still when I walked in. The servant who admitted me intimated that tea had been ready for quite some time. Tea for one. With my hand on my forehead I asked for the tea and aspirin to be sent to my room and went straight upstairs. The servant regarded me with furtive curiosity. I sensed no sympathy. Uncle Roger's household is of the distinctly male variety. I had not previously realised the servants might be resentful of the extra work I represented. I felt lonely and forlorn as I went upstairs to my elegant room.

On the tea tray, when it came, were three envelopes. One was your telegram from Nicosia:

Have a wonderful time, darling. Love to Thomas and don't let Roger bully you.

The second was a note from Uncle Roger:

No news yet. Have had to go out. The dinner has been cancelled. Try to get some rest.

The third envelope I held in my hand a long time before I dared to open it. It had a Turkish stamp and was addressed to me in Thomas's handwriting. You will hardly believe this, it was a love letter, very simple, very sweet, and written on one page of notepaper begged from an airport official. Here it is, because I'm putting everything in, and besides, I want to copy it out.

Yesilkoy – midnight

Dearest, dearest Helena,

I just can't believe you are really here, going to bed now, in that stageset bedroom at your uncle's. He must have had an actress in mind when he designed that guest room. I can think of a setting that will suit you much better, you know, the kind of thing known as the main bedroom, in the sort of apartment that is rented furnished by second secretaries and their wives. I believe that wives always change the curtains and bedspreads and rearrange the furniture. Will you do that, darling? You needn't on my account for I won't be looking at the décor.

The plane is late, which is why I've had time to scrounge this notepaper. I thought it would be mad and silly to write to you when I don't have to, so you'll get a surprise you are not expecting. Besides, I might as well be writing to you as sitting here thinking about you anyway.

Driving out here I thought Istanbul must be the most beautiful city in the world, even without moonlight. I kept remembering all sorts of funny little places to take you. Then I'd have a laugh at myself because I'd only be imagining your red hair against some new background, such as the harem in the Seraglio where hardly anybody goes. There are a couple of places quiet enough to kiss you.

On Sunday I think we will take the trip to the Isles des Prince. It's a fabulous place, I'll show you Russia across the water. Five more minutes. I'll put this in the box. It's a funny thing, I can't get over you being so interested in Rupert Augustinian. He has always interested me too. On my side it's probably the fascination of the legends that grow up around some of these types. But it could hardly be that for you. We'll go and eat there again sometime. I promise.

Goodnight, my sweet, sweet dreams. This is for tonight. Tomorrow night, I'll tell you myself too, only not this way.

I'll phone you for breakfast, if I can wait that long.

Your Sir Galahad in glasses,

Thomas

With the letter under my pillow, I went to bed. It was, of course, too early for sleep. I expected to get up again, driven by my sorely shattered nerves to walk the floor in mental agony. Instead, I slept almost immediately. It was only in the morning, when I was completely refreshed, that I decided to be the nervous type, frightened and ill.

My third day in Istanbul I read about Istanbul. I explained to Uncle, when he eventually came up to see why I missed breakfast, that I really felt too wretched to get up; that I couldn't possibly see anybody or answer questions, unless of course it would help Thomas, then perhaps I could struggle up if it was urgent and absolutely essential.

Uncle Roger was solicitous, so much so that I suspected his relief at finding me incapacitated and incapable of causing further complications.

'Your mother never had the sense to stay in bed,' he told me. 'She always kept going until she dropped, and she always dropped at three in the morning, when no doctor could be found.'

He had tripped over the telegram, which had fallen on the floor, so he had a right to be excused for such early-morning bitterness. 'I suggest a doctor look at you, Helena, just in case.'

'If you insist, Uncle Roger. But it isn't necessary, I'm only ill from wanting Thomas. It's the terrible strain. I'm exhausted with worry. In a day or two I'll be able to take hold again.' My voice trailed off in a sniff.

Uncle Roger went out with another kind of sniff, which he courteously attempted to suppress. He returned with my breakfast tray and a severe-looking upstairs maid of uncertain years. He told me she was the wife of one of the servants and would be near enough all day to answer my bell. We would see, he said, how I was by early evening and leave the question of a doctor until then. Meantime, was there anything else he could do for me before he left for the city?

'I'd appreciate something to take my mind off Thomas, if you could manage it for me, Uncle Roger.'

'Books, you mean. I'll take a look downstairs.'

'No, something lighter than that,' I said with a groan. 'Magazines or some books on Istanbul – you know, books for tourists about the Seraglio and the Isles des Prince and places like that. I may never be able to see the places now, Uncle Roger.'

'I think you will, Helena,' Uncle Roger said tartly, and then relented. 'I haven't much time this morning to go shopping. This business with the police and Thomas may occupy a good bit of time.'

'Oh, I didn't mean you to go and buy them, Uncle Roger – oh, I wouldn't think of that – I just thought maybe Joe Osman could get them.'

He considered my contrite, apologetic face. 'Well, I suppose Joe could get something after he drops me, and run them back.'

'That would be very kind, Uncle Roger. I'm sure he'd know what to buy. Anything he brings will do.'

Uncle favoured me with a glance of combined pity and suspicion. Girls of my age and disposition are foreign to him, I suppose, below the surface. Yet I know he is fond of me, he always has been. A schoolgirl appreciates an uncle who never forgets her birthday or Christmas or a graduation present. I favoured Uncle Roger with a sad smile and reached out a limp hand towards him.

'Dear Uncle Roger,' I said. 'You have always been so good to me.'

Completely baffled, he departed.

Osman did not bring me the books. The maid brought them in. I did not go out of my way to be pleasant to her, pretending instead to be in need of sleep. She opened the parcel and put the contents on a chair she drew up beside the bed. Then I waved her away with a gesture I intended to be as full of authority as the raising of Augustinian's hand had been to Osman. However, the maid retired no further than a chair just outside my open bedroom door. She seemed to have nothing else to do. She must have been hired especially for my benefit.

A prisoner was I? A prisoner in my own uncle's house, being spied upon by a nasty woman? But I was in bed, I reflected, at Mr Augustinian's suggestion – and by my own will, so I decided I might as well look at the books. The top volume was called *The Empresses of Byzantium*. Directly beneath was a copy of the poems of Pierra Loli, in French, which looked surprisingly second-hand. I picked up *The Empresses of Byzantium* and began to discover that Istanbul had housed some truly remarkable women.

By noon of my fourth day in Istanbul the toes on my feet were cramped with inactivity, while my brain was full to bursting with the wonders of the city I was debarred from viewing in person. The glories of harem intrigue, Christian massacre, Muslim politics and international spy-rings had made of me a modern Mata Hari, anxious to be up and about her business.

I sat up in bed, told the maid I felt better and demanded lunch.

With lunch arrived Uncle Roger. 'So you are better,' he enquired, 'Or bored?'

'Both,' was my answer.

'If you are quite sure you are better, I will take you after lunch for a little drive. You need not wear a hat.'

'Uncle Roger, what is it? You have news. I know you have news. I know you have news. Where are we going?'

'Mr Wilton and Ferguson plus two policemen are downstairs, Helena. We are going with them to establish the identity of a patient in a hospital.'

'Oh, Uncle Roger, a hospital, oh my God, not Thomas!'

'Pull yourself together, Helena. I said a hospital not a morgue. They think the patient is Thomas, but you're not to count on it. The man is unconscious, drugged they suggest, and had no papers on his person whatsoever. This kind of thing often happens in Istanbul.'

'I'll dress, I'll dress this minute.'

'Stay where you are. Eat your lunch or you don't go. The maid will get your clothes and help you dress as soon as you have finished.'

'Don't go, Uncle Roger. Tell me more while I eat. Tell me everything you know.'

'Yesterday I went to look at a man. It wasn't Thomas. I didn't think it would be Thomas by the description so I didn't tell you. Today the police are certain it is. They picked up Wilton and Ferguson and came straight over here. That's all I know. In case it is Thomas I would like to suggest, Helena, that you are more co-operative than you were the last time, for Thomas's sake, if not for mine.'

'Yes, Uncle Roger.'

'For example, you might hand over a letter that you received with a Turkish stamp on it the day before yesterday. Withholding information in a case like this is a criminal offence. Who was the letter from?'

'Who told you I got a letter?'

A sort of suppressed fury took hold of Uncle Roger. When he spoke his voice was rigid with anger and some other emotion that I could not fathom. 'That is not the point. The point is you did get a letter and as far as I have been given to understand, you do not know anyone else in Istanbul besides Thomas and myself – except that fool of a son of Karvies, and although he seemed capable of it, he could not have written you a letter you received in the post some hours after he left us. Who wrote that letter, Helena?'

It seemed to me that if I did not answer, Uncle would explode. I was frightened. I had never seen him like this. 'Thomas wrote it, Uncle Roger.'

'Thomas.' The name left his lips like the last expulsion of air from a deflated balloon. I couldn't look at him. I swallowed, without tasting and with difficulty, a mouthful of sticky rissole.

Then Uncle Roger said, 'A letter from Thomas is evidence.'

I thought it strange that he did not doubt me further.

'It was written before he disappeared.'

'Why? You were here.'

'He wrote it at the airport, before the plane came in with the bag on it.'

'Good heavens! I'll have to ask you to give me that letter at once, Helena.'

'I can't give it to you, Uncle Roger. It's a private letter.'

'It will have to be given to the police, Helena, private or otherwise.'

'It's a love letter, Uncle Roger. No more and no less. Thomas did not know he was going to be kidnapped with the bag!' I cried indignantly.

'I do not advise you to use the word kidnapped, Helena. There has been no proof as to how Thomas disappeared.'

'Uncle Roger. Let me get dressed so we can go now. If you insist, I'll show you the letter when we get back. Then you'll see that it's only a little love letter from Thomas to me.'

He stood in the room irresolute, looking at the floor, the bed, anywhere but at me. 'I have never been able to win,' he said then. 'Never.'

At that moment his eye was arrested by the pile of books. Like a hawk, he fell upon them and seized the poems of Loti.

'Where did you get this book?' he asked accusingly. 'Did Thomas give this to you too?'

'No. Mr Osman brought it with the others.'

'The fool,' my uncle said. 'The fool. I won't have you reading such rubbish.' He walked to the window, opened it, and with unaccountable viciousness, threw the book out.

'I haven't read it!' I said, appalled more than angered. 'I can't read French. But I don't suppose poor Mr Osman knew that.'

'Get your clothes on and come down,' was Uncle's command. 'God knows how much I hope this man will be Thomas.' He strode out of the room furiously, without closing my door. I heard him slam the door to his own room down the hall, a sanctuary I had never entered.

'I'll just go in there one day,' I thought to myself, with equal fury. 'I'll just go in there and see what I can see. He's got a worse temper than I have!'

The sombre-faced maid came to the door and regarded me placidly as I stood by the bed in my pyjamas.

'I'll dress myself, thank you,' I said tartly, and walked towards her to close the door. She stepped back, seeing my intention, and I distinctly saw her lips twitch as if she was restraining a smile, but she lowered her eyes and bowed gravely.

'Humph,' I thought. 'She's probably Osman's wife for all I know. As soon as I see Thomas by myself I'm going to tell him to get me out of here. I'll suggest we get married right away, promotion or no promotion.'

It didn't occur to me for a moment to doubt that the man I was going to see was Thomas. More than that, I felt quite sure that it was Rupert Augustinian who had found him and put him there. That being so, I reflected, the less I had to say driving to the hospital, the better. I put on the blue dress again, having decided it was not my colour, that I looked thin in it; wasting away, I hoped. A lack of lipstick was a sure guarantee that I would suck my wan, pale lips with the nervousness engendered by a half-dressed feeling. Then I descended, ahead, I hoped, of Uncle Roger, to throw myself on the sympathy of the delegation waiting below. Uncle was already with them, however and we started out at once.

The man in the bed was Thomas. Only when I saw him I felt exactly the way I had hoped I looked. In fact, it was all I could do for a minute not to faint. Uncle held my arm on one side and Mr Wilton supported me on the other.

Thomas was unconscious and his head above the eyes was swathed in bandages. He was not in a private room and I had heard him groan behind the screens that surrounded him even before I reached him.

'It's Pringle all right,' Mr Wilton said, and someone put a chair behind me and I dropped into it, level with poor Thomas's head.

Somebody said, 'He's coming round. We can't question him here. Isn't there a private room available?' The conversation switched suddenly into Turkish, but I only stared in consternation at Thomas's grey face. He groaned again and his body shuddered a little. I took his hand between my own and sucked in my breath. I think when I heard Thomas groan that I really knew for the first time all the things that could have happened to him. Nausea swept over me and I groaned too.

Mr Wilton put his hand on my shoulder. 'Take it easy, Miss Martine,' he said. 'It's not as bad as it looks. The doctor says he thinks Thomas was hit on the head and fell, but the injuries are not serious. He has been rather heavily drugged. But he will recover. Mr Ferguson is seeing about getting him moved into a private room.'

'Poor Thomas,' I whispered. 'Oh, poor Thomas. How did he get here, Mr Wilton?'

'On the back of a Galata Jew. The man said he picked him up in the gutter. It seems people thought he was drunk. He had been on the street for some time. The Jew brought him here.'

All I could say was, 'Poor Thomas, poor, poor Thomas.'

Then Uncle Roger went away and Mr Wilton went away. I sat in a kind of stupor, listening to angry voices, the loudest of which was Uncle Roger's in the corridor. A door banged shut, which was strange in a hospital, but it left me alone with Thomas. I sat there for an hour, or perhaps it was only a minute or even a year, with my stomach turning over and over. Then Thomas opened his eyes and to my amazement said, in a queer, thin voice, 'They took the bag, Helena, they took the bag. Got to get it back. Done for if I don't get it back.'

'Thomas,' I whispered, 'Oh, Thomas darling. You're safe now. You're going to be better.'

But he passed out again, his eyes closed against me. A nurse came in. She pushed me out of the way. Thomas began to be sick. A doctor came in. They took no notice of me, either the doctor or the nurse. I stood with my back against the screen, gripping the chair with both hands.

Finally, another nurse came in and spoke to the doctor. He nodded his head. She led me, unwilling and protesting, out of the ward into the corridor. But having reached the corridor I stood firm and would go no further. Whatever she was trying to explain to me in Turkish I could not understand and I would not leave Thomas. Shaking her head, she left me and when she came back again she was with Osman.

'He has come,' he said to me in English. 'I took the book to him and he has come.'

Osman had not driven us to the hospital. What was he talking about? Was it Thomas?

'My fiancé is very ill,' I said. 'I will not go away from here. I must stay with him.'

'I will give him the message.' Osman said, and walked away.

I caught up with him in the corridor. 'Where are you going?' I said.

He turned and looked at me strangely out of his peculiar eyes. 'To give Augustinian the message. You cannot come. You cannot come. Your fiancé is much too ill.'

Dumbfounded, I stared at the man and let him go away again. I went back to the door into the ward and stood there waiting. People stared at me, a pale, thin European girl with red hair, as they went past. After a few minutes the nurse came out from behind the screens that surrounded Thomas. The doctor followed her. He nodded to me and the nurse gestured that I should go in.

'Helena,' Thomas said, and knew me and smiled.

We were left for perhaps ten minutes alone together and I wasted the first five. Then I whispered to Thomas not to mention Rupert Augustinian, no matter what happened, until I had a chance to tell him all the things that had happened to me.

'Be sick as long as you can, Thomas. It will work, I'm sure. Feel sick if they ask questions.'

'That will be easy, darling,' Thomas said. 'My God, they must have hit me with a mattock. I'm in a fix, Helena. Do you still want me without the promotion or even a job? They got away with the bag. I never knew what happened.'

'I know, darling. It's terribly complicated. Just you get better and I'll have you any old way. They'll all be back soon. They'll want to ask questions when they get you out of here into a private room. There's Uncle and Mr Wilton and Mr Ferguson and—'

'Ferguson, my God.'

'And two Turkish policemen. Who's Ferguson, Thomas?'

'Only MI5. But don't let on I told you. I wonder what the hell was in that bag.' And Thomas groaned again. His eyeballs turned upwards and the skin around his mouth went a sickly green. He was violently sick again.

The nurse came once more and then the doctor, and after more time, Uncle Roger and the other men. The doctor went out from attending Thomas to speak to them, but he was back almost immediately and with him Uncle Roger, who led me gently to the corridor once more.

'We had to go to police headquarters, Helena,' my uncle told me, 'to get permission to have Thomas moved to another hospital. The police here would not accept Wilton's authority.'

Mr Wilton, with Ferguson, joined us, followed by the two members of the Turkish police.

'We have a single room for him and he'll be moved as soon now as it can be arranged,' Mr Wilton told me with displeasure. 'As if he could be left here.' He waved his hand vaguely, indicating the ward that held Thomas. 'If you'll come along now, Miss Martine, we will drive you with your uncle to the hospital where Thomas will be admitted.'

'No,' I said quite definitely. 'I will go in the ambulance with Thomas.'

'I'm afraid that won't be possible, Miss Martine,' Ferguson said bluntly. 'I will go with him and he will also be accompanied by this police officer.'

I looked Mr Ferguson straight in the eye.

'I won't leave Thomas,' I said. 'If you try to make me I'll scream.'

'Helena,' Uncle said harshly. 'Don't speak like that.'

'My dear Miss Martine,' Mr Wilton began, as if to persuade me, and then changed his mind.

'I will not leave Thomas, Mr Wilton. He needs me. He knows I'm here. I'll go with him.'

Mr Wilton consulted the man Ferguson, and Ferguson in turn the Turkish policemen. Then they all approached my uncle.

'Your niece is overwrought, sir,' Ferguson said to him. 'We suggest you take her home. We will send a car to bring her to the hospital this evening.'

'No,' I said.

Uncle Roger looked defeated. 'You can try ordering her not to scream if you wish, Mr Ferguson,' he said. 'It is quite useless for me to do so.'

They stared at me speculatively, you know how men do sometimes, and I backed away from them into the ward again. The nurse beckoned me. Thomas was relieved temporarily of nausea. I went to his side and sat down. He looked very weary, but his pallor was better and he managed to smile weakly.

'Poor Helena,' he said. Then, 'Hello, Sir.'

I turned to glare at Uncle Roger at my shoulder and said to Thomas quite loudly and distinctly, 'You are going to be taken to another hospital, Thomas, where you will have a room to yourself. I'll come with you in the ambulance.'

'Good girl,' Thomas whispered. 'I can't see a damn thing past the foot of the bed. They broke my glasses.'

'Mr Wilton is here too, Thomas, as well as Uncle Roger and Mr Ferguson,' I told him. 'It is only because you've been so ill, Thomas, that your eyes are blurred. You'll see better in a few minutes.'

'Knocked my glasses off before they hit me,' Thomas muttered.

'So you didn't see them?' Ferguson snapped from the door.

'What was that?' Thomas said.

'Nothing, dear. Please don't worry. Just wait a little while and then you'll be able to talk to Mr Wilton.'

Thomas turned his head towards me and closed his eyes.

Mr Wilton said kindly, 'We'll wait outside, Miss Martine. Come on, Ferguson.'

My uncle stayed with me until Thomas was put onto the stretcher and loaded into the ambulance. I climbed in and sat on the bench beside him. Across from me sat an orderly, and in the front seat, beside the driver, rode one of the Turkish policemen. We drove out through the hospital gates into a narrow street. At the end of this street the ambulance was stopped. The policeman got out. There was a murmuring of voices, a sinister sound when you are terrified and cannot see what is happening. I held Thomas's hand and we stared into each other's eyes. Then the policeman got in again and we drove off. When we stopped a second time we were in the driveway of another hospital, where the doctor was American. Thomas was admitted and put into a private room on the first floor. Until he was settled I waited in the reception room. While I was there the driver of the ambulance came in and handed me a note, which I put straight into my handbag as soon as I had read it. I showed the note to Thomas in the moment I had alone with him, before Uncle came and brought me back to this house. I am in my room now and I have been writing this letter ever since I retired after dinner.

Tomorrow I will be visiting Thomas in the afternoon and the evening. During these visiting hours, which are all Thomas will be allowed tomorrow, I do not expect we will be alone, but my presence will protect him from the questioning he dreads. I am taking to Thomas all that he needs from his rooms. It is impossible to say how long he will remain in the hospital. While he is there he has promised to write a letter, which I will enclose, if I can, with this one addressed to you. The day after tomorrow, when Mr Wilton and the man Ferguson and the police begin their questions, I will not be present, even though Thomas may need me desperately. He is very wan and pale and does not want me to go where I must. He has begged me not to go. Poor Thomas, I love him so dearly. I would die rather than hurt him. Yet it is as much for his sake I go as for my own.

The writing on the note I received is small and precise, but you will notice the brief message is not printed:

'On the day which follows tomorrow let the patient sleep. Maria will be waiting.'

From Thomas, With Patience

There are more ways than a man would believe possible of asking the same question, even though every way can only produce the same answer. The questions can be said to have come mainly from Ferguson, abetted if not aided by Wilton and the one single answer from me.

'Someone bumped me, my glasses were knocked off. Then I blacked out. That's all I know.'

'You came round?'

'In a dark place, tied up. Then I blacked out again.'

'Sick?'

'Not even time to be sick.'

'You'll have to do better than that, Pringle. Have you any idea who knocked you out?'

'No.'

'You saw nobody coming towards you?'

'No.'

'Yet you say you weren't alone at the terminus.'

'No.'

'How many people were in the waiting room?'

'I don't know. I didn't notice them much. I was writing a letter.'

'Who to?'

'My fiancée.'

'You had only just left Miss Martine. You planned to see her in the morning.'

'Yes.'

'Then why were you writing a letter to her?'

'To fill the time in.'

'Did you post it?'

'Yes.'

'She did not say she received it, Pringle.'

'Why should she?'

'We asked her uncle to check on her mail. She received a telegram from her mother, nothing else. Did you perhaps address it to her through a mutual friend?'

'No.'

'Was there any reason why you did not want her uncle to know she received a letter from you?'

'No.'

'Then why, if you sent it to his address, did she not admit she had received it?'

'I haven't asked her.'

'What was in the letter, Pringle?'

'It was purely a love letter, Ferguson. I suppose she didn't want it handed round. Would you?'

'You didn't send that letter by hand?'

'No.'

'By a friend?'

'No.'

'What were you doing at Augustinian's?'

'Having dinner.'

'What else?'

'What else would I be doing except talking to Helena?'

'And Augustinian?'

'I don't know Augustinian.'

'Why was he joking with you then?'

'Why would he be joking with me? I told you I don't know him.'

'Then he wasn't joking with you?'

'No.'

'Your fiancée said he was.'

'Look here, Ferguson, I'm trying to be co-operative. It happens I'm just as concerned as you are about what happened. I was responsible for the bag. What are you getting at?'

'Your story and Miss Martine's don't tally, Pringle.'

'Because she didn't hand over a love letter? You're a bit hard. You might consider that my fiancée had arrived in Istanbul for the first time in her life at 3 p.m. the afternoon all this happened. I worked all that day and picked her up to take her to dinner at night.'

'Why Augustinian's?'

'Peace, Ferguson. Quiet! My fiancée to myself! We only had the time after I left work until the time I went out to pick up the bag. We were by ourselves in Augustinian's, all by ourselves, didn't know a soul and we sat and talked about getting married next Easter. Augustinian noticed two completely absorbed love-birds in his establishment, and true to whatever romantic legend clings around him, took it into his head to wish us goodnight. He suggested I take Helena to see the view from Ayub the following night, when the moon was full. That is exactly all that happened at Augustinian's. Now will you tell me why you link up my hit on the head with Augustinian? You boys are always said to have a reason.'

'Roger Atherton, your fiancée's uncle, is involved in some way with Augustinian. His chauffeur drove to Augustinian's the day you were found.'

My position, it will be seen, was becoming increasingly difficult. If they were trailing Osman, Roger Atherton's chauffeur, they were trailing Helena and Helena thought, in fact she was sure, that Rupert Augustinian was responsible for my rescue.

No doubt the Embassy, through Ferguson, thought Augustinian responsible, not for my rescue but for my disappearance. Let alone the disappearance of the bag.

Nobody wished more than I did that I had not taken Helena to Augustinian's.

'Do you mind telling me, Ferguson,' I said, 'just what there is to know about Augustinian? Everybody seems to know considerably more than I do and I'm the most involved. What have you got on Augustinian? And what was in the bag of interest to him?'

'For a sick man you are asking a lot of questions and not giving many answers, Pringle.'

I appealed to Wilton. 'Look here, Sir,' I said. 'I'm sorry but I really am in the dark. I must know now, what was in the bag, what they were after.'

'There was nothing official in the bag – only private letters, including the one for you. I phoned Nicosia.'

'It must have been from my fiancée's mother.'

'Does she have the right to use our bag?' Ferguson interjected.

'No.'

'Then why should you think she should use it?'

'There's nobody else I know there, except Jenkins. He met me when I went to meet my fiancée. He would have said if the letter had been from him.'

'Does Jenkins know your fiancée's mother?'

'Yes, of course.'

'I see.'

I saw too. I saw that every time I opened my mouth I implicated somebody, which was a frightening enough thought, without knowing as well that every word I spoke involved myself and Helena even further.

'You don't see,' I snapped back at Ferguson. 'As you point out, it couldn't have been my fiancée's mother using our bag and it wasn't Jenkins, so I don't have any idea who the letter was from.'

'Are you expecting a visit from your fiancée this afternoon?'

'No.'

'Why? She was here twice yesterday.'

'So today she's tired out. So am I.' I turned my head wearily on the pillow and closed my eyes. My head under the bandages throbbed with reverberations like a hammer on a nail.

'She wouldn't be going to see Augustinian?'

'Augustinian, Augustinian. Why the hell would she be going to see Augustinian?'

I wished fervently that I knew because without doubt Helena was going to see Augustinian. Only I didn't know when or why. I only knew that, in spite of everything I said, in spite of my arguments, even my pleading, she was going to see Augustinian because of a note he had sent her.

'You ought to have some idea why,' Ferguson said.

I groaned and Wilton suggested to Ferguson that I had had enough.

'I'll take a smoke,' Ferguson said. 'Until Atherton comes. Be in the corridor if you want me.'

Wilton sat for a while without speaking. Then he said, 'I'll do all I can for you, Thomas. If there's anything you think I ought to know in confidence, spill it out.'

'It's complicated, Wilton,' I said gratefully. 'Damn complicated. The truth is I know nothing except a number of odd facts that don't fit. Helena also seems to know odd facts that don't fit.'

'Such as?'

'Such as her discovery that her uncle hates Augustinian and her belief that Augustinian rescued me.'

Wilton said nothing for a moment. When he spoke again, his voice held the sharpness of a sudden decision. 'He did,' he said.

'What did you say, Wilton?'

'The man who brought you in worked in Augustinian's kitchen. The police recognised him.'

'But they said I was found in the gutter.'

'My opinion is, Thomas, that Augustinian let the word get around that you'd better be put in some gutter, and a Galata gutter too, where one of his Jews could find you.'

'In that case he had nothing to do with kidnapping me.'

'That's my theory. But not Ferguson's.'

'What is Ferguson's?'

'I can't tell you that. I've told you my theory hoping you can throw some light on why your fiancée knew Augustinian would find you.'

'I wish I could, Wilton. I don't understand it at all. I know for a fact that Helena had never met Augustinian until the night I took her there for a meal. I myself had never had a word with him before he wished us goodnight. But he made an impression on Helena. I don't know why. Has Augustinian ever been out of Istanbul, can you tell me that, Wilton?'

'He hasn't been out of Istanbul for twenty years. Before that nobody ever knew where he was. That's why the police have a check on him.'

'Well, Helena is only twenty years old and this is the first time she's ever been in Istanbul or any part of Turkey. That proves Helena couldn't have known Augustinian previously.'

'It doesn't prove anything, Thomas, certainly not in connection with Rupert Augustinian.'

He was right. It didn't prove anything. I couldn't tell Wilton how sure Helena was that she had seen Augustinian before. She couldn't have pretended everything she said on that night. I had to trust her. It had to be Helena rather than all the others. I couldn't doubt Helena. Yet doubt was creeping in.

To waylay it, not to face it, I asked Wilton about Augustinian and he told me the little he knew. Rupert Augustinian was said to have a stranglehold on both Armenians and Jews. It was, Wilton thought, something to do with the Spanish Civil War. Augustinian was married to a Galata Jewess. It was her house they lived in, her house in which the restaurant was located. Some said she owned the whole street. For years, odd things occurred in that street. People and treasures disappeared. Augustinian sat in his restaurant year in year out, always questioned, never involved. Wilton suggested he must be the master of the perfect alibi. He certainly had it in the only case about which Wilton had full details, referring to Nazi treasure that was to pass through Istanbul from a hide-out in Spain, on its way to an undercover organisation that harboured escaped Nazi party members in Egypt. The loot was traced as far as the harbour in Istanbul where it disappeared on the backs of Galata Jews. Turkish and Allied authorities were after it, the Germans desperate men, but Istanbul absorbed the spoils. It was useless to question the long line of Spanish Jews who left the camps in Europe shortly afterwards and passed through Turkey on their way to make new lives in Israel, or the Armenians who measured gold in the perfectly balanced miniature scales of their profession. The authorities traced the German agents and delivered them to justice but nobody recorded the stolen goods. Rupert Augustinian sat as usual at the same table in his restaurant. Each night his wife had joined him for an hour. He was always available and never really available at all.

'Why does he wear those clothes?' I asked Wilton.

'I asked that myself,' Wilton said. 'Nobody seems to know. Before he settled here he was not only in Spain but in Egypt and Palestine, in Baghdad, Damascus and the desert. Lots of his kind take to the flowing robes, T. E. Lawrence types.'

The nurse came in and Wilton went out. When he returned Ferguson was with him and so was Helena's uncle, Mr Atherton.

'Where's Helena?' I asked Mr Atherton. 'Hasn't she come with you?'

'No,' her uncle said. 'I couldn't let her have the car today. I needed my chauffeur. I won't risk having her take a taxi. She's resting and furious. You have my sympathy, Thomas. My sister has spoiled Helena. I suppose it was to be expected. Ferguson, I'm a busy man. Could we get on with business? You wanted me for a discussion here.'

'Did your niece get a letter from Pringle the day after he disappeared?'

Mr Atherton hesitated only for the fraction of a minute. 'No,' he said. 'As far as I know, she didn't. My servants would have told me if she had.'

'You asked them?'

'I did.'

'How long have you had your chauffeur, Mr Atherton?'

'Six years.'

'He came to you from Augustinian?'

Atherton jumped. 'He did not. If he had anything to do with Augustinian I would fire him immediately. He came from Idirna, his home town.'

'He may have been to Idirna, Mr Atherton,' Ferguson snapped, 'but he certainly worked for Augustinian before he worked for you.'

Mr Atherton's mouth contracted.

I don't know Mr Atherton very well as he was only an acquaintance of mine from Istanbul staying in the same hotel in London when he introduced me to Helena. I'll always be grateful to him for that, no matter the outcome of this fiasco. I felt sorry for him, standing there trying to control his temper. Ferguson is big and tough. His voice rasps in that irritating cross between cocky and Cockney that raises the ire in one. Ferguson went right on with the business in hand according to Ferguson and made Mr Atherton look like a dapper little fool.

'Your chauffeur dropped you here,' Ferguson said. 'And drove off. Where did he go?' He punctuated with stops his remarks, which were irritatingly slow.

'To put an office delivery in Curzah's, not that it's any of your damn business,' Atherton snapped.

'Gentlemen,' Wilton said

Ferguson went right on. 'I suggest, Atherton, that your chauffeur went back to your house, picked up your niece and took her to Rupert Augustinian.'

'I don't believe your rotten insinuations.'

'Mister Atherton,' Wilton said, 'Mr Ferguson is doing his duty, no more and no less. Believe me, he is not insinuating anything. In some way your niece is connected with Rupert Augustinian. This is clear to all of us, including her fiancé. So is Osman, your chauffeur.'

'How?' Roger Atherton said. 'Tell me how.'

'The day Pringle was found, Osman delivered a parcel at Augustinian's. It was one of Augustinian's men who carried Pringle to the hospital. The ambulance that brought him here was stopped, and later the driver of the ambulance handed a letter to your niece. The driver of the ambulance was an Armenian called Marcasian. Do you want to know more, Atherton?'

Mr Atherton turned to me then with a strange expression, like a schoolboy trapped in the middle of a melodramatic dialogue in which he was the hero. He looked both deflated and highly excited, two little red spots burned on his cheeks. His mouth was twitching under his moustache.

'Thomas,' he demanded. 'Do you believe Helena is at Augustin- ian's?'

'I don't know, Sir,' I said. I was telling him the truth and I was telling him a lie and he knew it.

'If Helena is there, Thomas,' he said, 'she will not come back to my house. Do you hear? She will not come back to my house.'

'If Helena is there,' I said, 'she has a good reason to be there and I be- lieve that. So should you.' But I was worried and sick with a dread that was greater than the pounding of my head.

'We'll go there,' Ferguson said. 'Now.'

'I will save you the trouble of the journey perhaps, gentlemen. She is there. I have left her with my wife. She is clever, is she not, Roger? She has recognised my wife from your painting.' The voice was soft and flowing, yet distinct.

Augustinian stood just inside the door. Stiff and straight, he dwarfed the other men in the room. Behind him, at the level of his shoulder, was the solemn face of a Turkish policeman, the guard on duty in the vicin- ity of the door of my room.

'You will be glad to know that the bag that was lost has been found. I have come to tell the young man.'

'You have it?' It was Roger Atherton who cried out.

'I do not have it,' Augustinian said. 'The police have it.'

'How do you know they have it?'

'I have friends.'

'Spies, that's what you have. Spies all over this city. Spies and sneaks.'

'I prefer to call them friends,' the soft voice purred.

I had been about to speak, but held my tongue, taking my cue from Wilton and Ferguson who were watching tensely. I saw Ferguson's hand move slightly.

Augustinian said, 'Mr Atherton is unarmed.' His voice was very low. We could have heard a pin drop in the room.

'You – you—' Mr Atherton spluttered, livid with fury.

'And I do not carry a gun.' Augustinian finished, without taking his eyes off Mr Atherton.

'Where was the bag found, Mr Augustinian?' Wilton asked him.

'In the gutter, I presume,' Rupert Augustinian replied, looking steadily at Mr Atherton's face.

The fight drained out of Mr Atherton and he regained control of himself. 'If you gentlemen will excuse me,' he said, 'I will go. I do not wish to remain in the same room with this man.'

'Osman is not back yet,' Augustinian said, still addressing Mr Atherton. 'You will have to wait. He will drive your niece home and then he will come for you.'

'No,' I said, in sudden horror. 'No, I do not want that. I want to see Helena. I want to see her here.'

'I will arrange that, Thomas,' Mr Wilton said immediately. 'I will be pleased to drive Mr Atherton home and bring Miss Martine back. As Mr Augustinian has come to visit you, Thomas, perhaps he will be kind enough to stay here until I return. Mr Ferguson, meanwhile, could take the opportunity to check the contents of the bag.'

There was no mistaking the authority in Wilton's voice. Ferguson and Atherton would accept it. Would Augustinian?

'I came to see the young man,' Rupert Augustinian said. 'I did not expect to find so many gentlemen. I will stay.'

'Wilton, I suggest Ferguson stay until we return,' Mr Atherton said.

'The bag must be checked, Mr Atherton,' Wilton replied. 'Mr Augustinian will be here when I return.'

'You believe that?' Atherton snapped.

'Certainly,' Wilton said, and the authority was there again. I knew then that Ferguson did not want to go. 'Mr Augustinian has given his word.'

Ferguson stalked out, pushing the policeman aside with a grunt in lieu of apology.

'I will bring your fiancée back, Thomas,' Mr Wilton said. He indicated that Atherton precede him to the door. Rupert Augustinian stood quite still, in the same spot as they passed him.

'Please sit, Mr Augustinian,' I said. 'If you wouldn't mind, on this side. It's easier on my head.'

He moved straight over and took the chair, lowering his great length stiffly into it so that he sat as he stood, quite erect, head and shoulders higher than another man would have been. I still had to look up to see his face.

'Tension is useless,' he said. 'It aggravates the pain.'

'I should be looking after Helena,' I said.

'It is impossible. She knows that, without doubt.'

'You didn't need to promise to stay,' I said irritably. 'Why did you?'

'You do not doubt I will remain? Yet you are full of doubts. What are you frightened of? Helena is in safe hands.'

'You know Wilton?'

'No more than I know you. I have had experience of men.'

'So has Wilton.'

'I observed that. Then there is Osman?'

'Atherton's chauffeur! God!'

'He was an Armenian refugee. He is clever and careful. For Helena, he would die.'

'Why?'

'Because he would die for me.'

'And why would you tell him to die for Helena?'

'She came to me,' he said. 'Her trust was unforeseen and touching. I do not know what sent her to me. But I am grateful.'

You, grateful to Helena. Mr Augustinian, how well do you know Helena? Have you met her before?'

'I saw her for the first time when you brought her to dinner in my restaurant.'

'But you know Roger Atherton?'

'He has not tolerated the sight of me for twenty years.'

'Is it true you found me?'

'It is true that I was fortunate enough to find you. I have lived for many years in Istanbul. I know where to look.'

'Then I owe my life to you.'

'You were a victim. I do not think it was intended that you should be harmed. Shall we say, rather, that it was necessary that you disappear with the bag. It is even possible that you were not expected to collect the bag.'

'It's my job.'

'But not, perhaps, the first night after the arrival of your fiancée.'

'What was in the bag?'

'I do not know. I have no interest in the contents of the bag.'

A strangely comfortable silence settled between us. For my part it was peopled with a past of unsolved mysteries. I had nevertheless become enlightened enough to be reasonably satisfied, in spite of the mysteries. I realised, as I lay in the silence, that the physical ache in my head was eased and my overwhelming personal concern about Helena, which had been superimposed over everything else, was gone. It came to me that there was reason for Osman to be willing to die for Augustinian and equal reason for Helena to trust him.

Also, it crossed my mind that I should be suspicious to be so lulled, but all I felt was relief, a kind of rest in the magnetism of the man. Yet I couldn't ask him more questions. We had come to the end of the questions. I felt like a small boy told the facts of life by his father, as far as the phase he was capable of understanding. Like the small boy, I would have to wait patiently until time passed to continue the conversation.

Of course, I could surmise in the meantime. I could even assume. My first assumption would be that Roger Atherton had once been in love with Rupert Augustinian's wife. That was, of course, what Helena had realised. I smiled inwardly. Trust Helena to get there first. As a mere male I accept women's intuition to the point where I would have been disappointed to find no signs of it in Helena. As far as I am concerned, she has to have everything.

I moved my head away from the sight of Rupert Augustinian. I was not being rude, nor was I restless. It was worse than that. The move was unconscious and unintentional. I was quite suddenly and inexplicably relaxing into a peaceful and natural sleep.

I awoke into the darkness of night, alone. The dim glow of the corridor light revealed the slumped shadow of the Turkish guard asleep on a wooden chair tilted against the open door of my room. Where Augustinian had been only the ghost of his presence remained. On my bedside table a shaft of light struck the photograph of Helena that I had asked her to bring from my flat, with the notepaper on which I write. I lifted the photograph and held it in my hands. Only the outline of her face was visible, the line of her chin, the cheekbone beneath her eye. I couldn't see her soft mouth, her pale fair skin or the glory of her hair. And I couldn't grasp the intangible spirit of Helena. The essence of what she was to me did not flow through from the picture into my hands and heart. The sweetness of Helena was not in the room. Only the presence of Augustinian was here, dominating the atmosphere with the truth of what I should have known.

The time is one half hour from midnight. I will have to wait until one. She asked me to write. So I am writing before I go and as I write I am making my plans.

Dictated by Maria

Helena has asked that I write to you and after I think of it many hours I have consented. She has talked a long time, Helena with me. She is using her hand for I do not write this twenty years she has been born. She sits very close and my darkness is lightened that she is near. She writes what I speak. It is better so. It is for her I write. You are full of fortune for this child has love, and that which goes or does not go in the natural way with love which is wisdom. She loves you and she loved instinctively Rupert, with trust and without knowledge. She has even love left over for me. She protests I put this. The credit for so much love is embarrassing to one so young, who thinks love is a special thing between a man and a woman that flows over into the channels around it, making the moat that protects it. You and I and Rupert are the moat that Helena needs to feel secure. It is for this I write, for it shall not be said that I, Maria, should be a gap or an empty place.

Is it not strange that we who were four with the glories of the world in our hands should have produced but one recipient, one vessel into which we can pour such dreams as we had? I have not seen Helena, but I have felt her hair and know well the brilliance and the glow for I envied it long enough. I have felt the bones of her brow and cheek that I have loved with equal ardour. So I have something too, which no one can deny me. And I have her recognition. She saw me as I was, when the joy was in me and the hate and the recklessness, and she knew me in spite of the hollow abyss of misery through which I have come. So

I have a share that is only mine. You will grant the share. You were always generous, too much so perhaps, although I thank my God for that. That was the difference between you and Roger. You shared pride but it was less than mine, in the end, and less than Rupert's. Now the pride has gone, out of all four of us. We had magnificence too, the wild sort, uncontrollable, violence that went with beauty and magnetism, intelligence and wit. We have spent all this – Roger in accumulating bitterness and wealth; Rupert and I in the international intrigue that is involved in dragging human flotsam from the jaws of destruction to die of their wounds in peace. And you spent all your talents in making one home after another, to bring up a little girl to the place where she would make a good wife to a fortunate man. Having reached this place, your generosity took you again, in spite of yourself. You could no longer keep what was not entirely yours. At the very moment when you were handing over your joy, in that instant when your all was becoming merely a second place, you wrote a letter. Now I write a letter I did not expect to write, from a heart I felt I no longer possessed.

Helena says that if I go on in this way I will have no sleep, as if one night of sleep more or less matters to me. But I accept her advice to please her. I will tell what has happened here tonight.

Life is quiet these days for Rupert and me, yet every evening we sit as we have for so many years at our corner table in the restaurant downstairs.

There was the beginning of all this, on the night when I knew that Rupert was not with me in spirit, although his chair was close. When I asked he told me he was looking at a boy and a girl at one of the tables, a boy and a girl who were lovers; the boy he had seen before, but the girl never. The girl had red hair.

It is not often when I am there that Rupert will speak to his clients. But he broke his habitual reserve that night and he spoke to the boy. There's a saying we have, 'So she has come'. He said that and he spoke of the moon at Ayub. It was all strangely tense. The boy spoke but the girl not a word.

The next day Rupert went to sit in the place he loved at Ayub. You will remember the place. Often in the first years of our marriage he would disappear with a book and I knew he would go there. Always when he went I was filled with grief and bitterness. But I could not speak. I could only wait until time relieved his agony. During the war he gave up Ayub. He was unsafe there and I was full of thanks. But the day after the girl with the red hair had greeted him without words he told me simply, 'I am going this day – to Ayub.' And I knew that after all these years there was a new distress in him and I was disturbed.

That night he was absorbed in misery so that his conversation was distant. I asked him if he was well, for there are days when he suffers much, and he answered me – 'Well, enough'.

When he took me upstairs, according to our custom, he said he was expecting Osman and prepared to go out again. But before he called old Sadi, who is still with me always when Rupert is not, he went to the bookcase and removed a book and when he went out he took the book with him. It was one he had not read to me, for I felt its empty place upon the shelf.

Was it one day, two days after perhaps, when Sadi came to me where I sit on the small balcony to listen to the sounds of the street, two floors below. 'Osman has come,' she said. 'He is urgent for the Master and has little time. The Master is not in his rooms.'

It was past the hour for the midday meal and not yet time for coffee. Rupert always joined me for the coffee unless he told me otherwise, but he had not yet come.

'Show Osman in,' I said, and rose up and entered the room through the long doors to receive him. You will remember the room. Nothing is changed. Every piece is in the same position. All that fascinated you is here. I ran my fingers over the latticed cupboards that intrigued you so much when you first visited my house. 'Don't ever change a thing, Maria,' you said. 'Everything fits so perfectly. Even the carpets look as if they have been here for a hundred years.'

I said to you, 'They have, there has just been this house for my family for two hundred years.' And you were astounded, and so too has Helena been astounded.

So I waited for Osman, standing between the divan and the beaten copper table in front of the little Goya that I used to hate and presently adored from long association.

Osman was very brief. He gave me a book for Rupert. He was nervous because he stumbled a little on the ottoman. He told me I was to give the book to Rupert as soon as he came in, give it with my own hands.

'Only a book,' I said. 'What book is it?'

'The poems,' Osman said. 'The Loti poems – he will know.'

'You will take no coffee, Osman? Then you will come again soon?'

He kissed my hand and stumbled twice as he went out. I held the book in my hands and I felt its cover gently because it was worn. The shape was a shape of the space I knew. I went over to the place and fitted the book. Then I returned to the table with the book in my hand and waited for Rupert. When he came in he greeted me with courtesy, as he always does. Time has not altered the gentleness of his manner to me.

But there was in me a cold, gripping fear, the spectre of something with which I could not cope. It hovered within me and forced itself into words. 'So, Rupert,' I said. 'You love again.'

He did not answer. I handed him the book, which he took from me in even deeper silence.

'There is a note inside, I felt it.'

'Osman brought the book?'

'Yes.'

He tore open the envelope. In the quiet of this room the paper rustled as he read. His voice said, 'I must go. The note is from Osman.'

'It is the girl with red hair,' I accused. I was trembling uncontrollably. I, Maria, so long passive, so long in my secluded valley, so safe with Rupert crippled even more than I.

'Maria,' Rupert said to me, then in Spanish, placing his hand on my hand. 'Poor Maria. Do not disturb yourself, foolish one. It is the girl with red hair, yes, but not as you think. She loves the boy who was with her that night. She is the niece of Roger Atherton.'

'Then I am still right,' I cried. 'Only it is worse. You still love.' Bitterly I began to weep, pressing my knuckled hands to my useless eyes.

'Maria,' Rupert said. 'You will listen to me. There is in this girl more than I can fathom. She was in trouble and she came to me. I will bring her to you.'

'I will not see her,' I wept. 'What could she be to me, her daughter and his niece? Go and be done with it, Rupert. Do what you must, but do not bring her to look in pity on my face.'

'She is very young, Maria. Younger than any you have had in this house since you came home to it.' There was in his voice a compulsion, a hidden communication that was almost a plea.

I was forced to respond. 'Bring her then,' I said roughly, and with passion. 'Bring her to look upon my incapacity.'

But when she came, my fear of her pity was as nothing compared to her fear of being in my house. It was her generous heart that brought her. She thought she was paying a debt to Rupert and she came in terror, against every principle of good sense that was in her. Against the threat of her uncle, and the advice of her fiancé. Against authority. When she shook my hand she was trembling with apprehension. Her fiancé had been hit on the head and kidnapped, found again to lay in a hospital, yet she had come. She had been warned of the mystery of the house of Augustinian, of the strange unnamed men who had passed through Istanbul, stopping only long enough to be seen in the vicinity of Galata for a matter of hours before they disappeared again. She was only a child, a product of a select English boarding school, and she had become the centre of such intrigue as she had merely read of in books and seen in cinemas. Every street in Istanbul she saw as a stranger, without the reassurance of familiar things.

I was unaccustomed to thinking of my house as a place of iniquity and apprehension, and therefore unbelievably touched by a generosity that admired its beauty unreservedly under such circumstances, flattered to be considered responsible for the beauty no matter what manner of intrigue I carried beneath the painted ceiling. I tried to put the child at her ease but it was impossible. I could feel her looking around, trying to find that which she could discuss without offending me. She was terrified yet fascinated. I could not allay the fear. I had been too long cut off, too isolated from any but the society of my own people. I was ingrown.

Then, quite suddenly, she picked up the tiny model of the dancer. You will remember. It stands alone on one compartment of the mashrabiya shelves. She was too restless to sit down and I knew from her voice where she was standing.

'You must have been a beautiful dancer.' Her voice held a note of high determination and the kind of youthful courage that dispenses with the falsity of useless words.

I was startled, which was natural, was it not, considering Rupert had told me she knew nothing of the past, that Roger would have her know nothing and that he, Rupert, in agreement preferred she remained unenlightened?

Osman had brought her, and Rupert had immediately left her with me. In an hour Osman would take her away.

In reply to my silence, she was as nervous as a trapped bird, and as voiceless as I for a little time. Then she pulled in her breath bravely and began again.

'I know you were a famous dancer,' she said. 'I know it because I recognised the painting in my uncle's study. I looked at the painting and I knew I had seen you before and I thought it was strange because I knew I had seen your husband before too. When I thought of that I knew you were the dancer in the portrait. Your hands were the same, and your head. But I don't know where I have seen him before. But I know him just the same. There's something.'

'The artist who painted me sketched his head quickly once. Very little time but he captured Rupert. Is that what it is you remember?'

'Yes,' she said immediately. 'Yes. I saw it only once when I was a little girl. It was in a book. How did you know?'

'Once, a long time ago, before you were born, my husband was in love with your mother.'

'And my uncle was in love with you,' she finished, and I heard her although her voice was no more than a whisper, a sigh in the leaves of a tree.

'Your mother stood once where you are standing now. It was she who brought Rupert to my house.'

'And Uncle Roger was here too.'

'He was here too.'

'How strange it is she did not tell me,' she said then. 'That she should have seen – all this – and let me come without knowing. It is not like her at all – I cannot understand. Will you tell me?'

'Will you come and sit beside me here? Will you let me touch you? Will you let me know what you look like? All the things in this room I know well because I have touched them so often they are intimate friends.'

'You do not like strangers in this room,' she said with quick perception.

'And you think I am wrong?'

'Why did you let me come?'

'Because Rupert asked me. Is that reason enough?'

'Yes, it is a good reason. I can understand it. But it is not the reason I would like to sit beside you and be like the other things in the room.'

'No?'

'No. It is because of what you told me about the picture and about my mother.'

'Yes?'

'You said he was in love with her, not that she was in love with him. That was hard for you.'

She sat down then on the carpet at my feet, so that the fresh young scent of her skin was in my nostrils and the silk of her hair under my hand. We talked for a long time, of many trivial things, before the strength was in me to touch her cheek. Then I knew.

Osman came to get her. She did not want to go. Her fear of going back to Roger's house was greater than the terror she felt when she came to mine. But she did not hesitate. Only quite suddenly she embraced me and I felt the tremor in her and was filled with compassion.

'You will come again?' I murmured.

'I don't know,' she said. 'I'll try. I'll never forget.'

She was gone and I sat in the seat of polished ebony. The hard throne, you called it, all studded as it is and inlaid with mother of pearl that tortured my meagreness like thorns. I sat there for hours, or was it a lesser span of time, before Rupert came in the door.

'She is long gone, Maria?' he said, comprehending how long I had awaited him there and yet asking a question that demanded an answer.

'Yes, she is gone,' I said. 'Osman came as you directed. But it was in my heart to keep her, for she trembled with fear. Is it fair, what you do to this child, Rupert Augustinian?'

'I did not know,' he said. 'Until tonight I was not sure. I have come from the hospital, Maria, where the boy sleeps. Her photograph was there on the table. When I saw it I could not doubt. So now I go to the house of Roger Atherton.'

'No, Rupert. No, no.'

'Will you have me wait until he comes here to kill me? My death is in his mind, Maria. I saw him tonight. There is violence in him.'

'This was what he had then, Rupert, this knowledge that he kept from us. It is this that enabled him to live in our shadow, though she would not?'

'It was he, Maria, who feared a letter in the stolen bag.'

'Is he discovered, Rupert?'

'I do not know. That is why I must go. The man Wilton knows what was in the bag. He will know what is missing from it. He will keep Helena with him. They did not return to the hospital. It is well the boy sleeps. Osman came for me. He waits below.'

'All of you lives again, Rupert.'

'This is why I must go. She must not be harmed, Maria. Nothing else matters.'

'I must come with you, Rupert.'

'There is no help in that. You are safe here, and secure. I would rather nothing is changed.'

'Yet I must come. Since I know I am responsible.'

So we went together, Rupert and Osman and I, to Roger's house. But not to the Atherton's house I knew. The perfume of you was long since obliterated by the sterile odourlessness of modernity. I knew that as I passed the portal, as Rupert and Osman guided me between them like a ghost whose feet were denied the firm reverberance of pressure on the stairs. We went in the back way, from the hill side, where the little gate opens by the ancient black key in the great wrought-iron lock. I went like a spectre to the scene of my disgrace, for I knew with an urgency that choked my breath how I had used Roger, to be near you, wanting the fire of your hair under my hand in deepening friendship. I knew how Rupert loved you, of course, how other men looked and loved you as a woman. That will always have been so. It will be so now and remain so when you are bent and grey. But I, as a woman, adored you, which was unique for me, whose only passion was my art. I was a woman loved as an artist which was as it should be, for it was really all I was. A dancer, a flame that danced and then went out to glow like a coal until it came alive to dance again. It was enough, more than enough for one life, but when I saw you I wanted more. I wanted to be like you. I wanted to be everything you were, to have everything you had. Even Rupert. I didn't want to be a dancer any more. I denied myself, my real self. How could you know this? You were the recipient of this obsession, who returned affection to me in friendship and trust, pleading with me not to go to Spain, not to use art as a weapon of war. You knew the difference between art and woman. Roger knew it too. Poor Roger. He was the only man who loved me entirely as an artist and woman combined, or rather as woman consumed by art. He asked for nothing more than to love me. He wanted no more than I was. I see now that he would have accepted cruelty, infidelity and harshness without question, without complaint. His love for me was composed of potential forgiveness. I alone should have brought out the best in him. But you, who through your own strength unwittingly denied him, he could not forgive, nor Rupert. I knew these things quite suddenly, going into his sterile house surreptitiously as the ghost of his love unlocking a secret gate. But because of Helena, who is living love as you were living love; because of Helena, who will not let me say another word, refusing to admit that love is torture if it is truly love, I will speak no more. She says there is no more to say and she is crying. Her hands are wet with her own tears as she holds the pen. I have said more than enough and will leave the rest to others, to Helena and to Thomas who is worthy of her. You knew he was, when you wrote to him did you not? Maybe you knew when you first met him. Helena laughs, happy again at the thought of you and Thomas. She will tell me why some time, she says, but not now. Now I must sleep. I will do as she asks. I am the child, secure again. Helena the mother, since last night.

Written by Roger Atherton, Under the Portrait

You should not have threatened. Even with your unpredictable code of values, you could have refrained. Some things drive a man too far.

After all, from the time she was born and before, I have done everything possible for Helena. She has wanted for nothing my money could buy and that without asking. It was even I who introduced her to Thomas Pringle. I planned to set her comfortably off with a generous marriage settlement. Thomas is not as perfect as Helena considers him to be, but he has made it apparent he wants her and none other. To the mother of any girl, Thomas would appear a good catch, combining a secure future with the steady sort of personal characteristics most women adore for their daughters, if not for themselves.

I invited Helena here in good faith. Certainly she expected I would. You must concede that as she is of a determined mind she might very well have come here anyway. It was much better that she come at my invitation, spend two weeks in my house, be taken shopping at my expense – especially considering the negligibility of her other resources. My idea was that she could plan her marriage with Thomas, marry him next Easter and go with him to his new posting in another part of the world. I suspected no danger in the arrangement. The last thing I expected was interference from you, and your first letter roused me to the fury that accounted for my telegram. For your telegram there is no excuse. Upon it lies the full responsibility. It will be of no use whatsoever to blame fate for the coincidence that Thomas should take Helena to dine at Augustinian's the night of her arrival. This should not have mattered. What did matter, and what can be called my inevitable misfortune, was Wilton's insistence on procedure that would not excuse Thomas from his duties even for one night, which was all that Thomas had asked for and I expected he would get.

My orders were to bring the bag so that I could remove your letters before having the bag dropped again in a gutter near the airport. This procedure, although unlawful, would not be unexpected in Istanbul. The price I offered for this service was too generous and the man I hired unscrupulously greedy. I was as sure of his greed as I was of your capability to write the letter. What else would you do after calling me 'Fool', having made up your mind to sacrifice Helena's future for the sake of a man like Augustinian? Even so, Thomas knocked down and the bag stolen would have meant no more than Thomas an assaulted hero. Thomas, however, chose to be more than a hero and hung on to the bag with the tenacity of a dead man's frozen fingers, which threatened my emissary's greed. He had been standing hidden as Thomas passed his car and threw the bag into it with Thomas attached. This forced my further implication. I agreed that Thomas be drugged further and hidden until at least two days after the bag was disposed of and found. The procedure, however, was reversed. Thomas was found before the bag was discovered. Augustinian found out where he was and had him put on the street, for he has spies everywhere. One of them I found in my own house.

At the hospital that now contains Thomas I was confronted with Rupert Augustinian. He has not changed much, except that his face has hardened and his body stiffened with age. He came to the hospital of his own free will to tell Thomas that the bag had been found and that Helena was with Maria; that Helena had recognised Maria from the portrait in front of which I sit as I write at my desk. Augustinian said my own chauffeur had driven Helena to Maria. I could have killed him then, but I did not have a gun. To know about Helena he must have been spying on me all of these years. He must have suspected the source of my wealth during the war, when I obliged a foreign power. You too suspected this, did you not, when for Helena's sake I divulged a bank balance you in your poverty could haughtily despise?

You, of course, can afford to be superior as the widow of Paul who gave his life for the cause, but I stayed on here, useless to the cause, a furtive little unwanted man searching for the means to hang on to the remnants of the family business. Staying in my rightful place, beating my memories down, I found a way to provide for you and Helena, whom I expected to return when hostilities ceased.

Not that I was successful in anything but the means of wealth. You would not return. I could not beat the memories down. I knew that tonight, sitting beside Wilton in the car, returning to face Helena. I know my whole life to be a memory. All I am is a sour, putrid black memory, up against the law because of one man – Rupert Augustinian who, with the aid of the only woman I ever wanted in my life, is still strong enough to try to take Helena from me. I am trapped. Wilton knows I stole the bag. I suspect he has also found out other things from Augustinian, whom he treated in my presence as a colleague and a gentleman.

Twenty years is a long time to hate a man like I hate Rupert Augustinian. It is too late to remember now your advice to sell out father's business and leave Istanbul. It is too late to recall how you begged and harassed me to re-establish myself in America. I was to make a new life, according to you. What with? He had Maria. She wanted him and she took him. She took what she wanted and she wanted Rupert Augustinian. Even with a bullet hole in his stomach and another woman in his heart. You would have taken him too, only you couldn't compete with Maria. You were more beautiful but she had more than beauty. She had fire instead of blood in her veins and her nerves were steel. You didn't know that after you left I tried desperately to see her, though I never succeeded. I crawled like a snake on my belly, I cringed and I cried but she would not answer my letters. I prowled around her house but instructions on the door denied me entrance.

She did not come out and she showed no pity. What was finished with her was finished. It was the same when she danced. She was a flame, sparking everything around her. When she stopped she went out like a light and the darkness was deeper than the oil beneath the sea. Well, she was a Jewess, but deeper than that, Spanish. During that last tour she danced in Spain, the secret police were after her, even then Gestapo dominated, but still she escaped. I never could find out how she escaped, though the city was full of gossip. All that mattered to me was that she came back and wouldn't see me and did not dance again. She poured all her wealth and all her soul into some rumoured bottomless pit for refugees with Augustinian.

Do you remember how he talked her into going to Spain? He was so eloquent, so dramatic, six-foot-four of the man magnificence. She was an artist and he turned her into a virago of Spanish obsession. I would have gone with her anywhere, putting her art above everything else, certainly above my own interests. We talked for hours, Maria and I, while she sat for her portrait. She wanted to go to South America, then Mexico, and after that New York. I imagined myself beside her, manager, lover, husband, friend, whatever she wanted. But she ended by wanting Spain, only Spain, because Augustinian had been to Spain and she was Spanish. Even though he did not want her, though he sat night after night for three months with his eyes on you, she went to Spain. She sacrificed herself for him.

I keep remembering your face the night you got his letter; the night they returned from Spain. Even then I had to envy you the letter, for I had no communication. She was home but she cared too little for me, for all I had offered, even to write.

You looked at me with those tremendous eyes of yours, which you insisted on making up with kohl, although God knows they didn't need it. Helena did exactly the same thing the other day and looked positively ridiculous.

The skin around your mouth was blue-white.

'We've had everything we wanted all our lives, Roger. Now we haven't. Rupert has married Maria.'

You wouldn't tell me any more that was in your letter. There were no reasons given, you said, but you believed he had a reason, though you wouldn't ask him for it. You accepted his word. You sent no answer to his letter.

'But what in God's name will we do?'

'Do? Leave here, of course. Get away. Sell up. Depart. What else? I'll get married.'

'Married? Get married?' I think I screamed the words.

'Why not? I was engaged to Paul Martine. I'll cable him I'm coming back to London.'

'You broke it off. You told him there was someone else.'

'I know, but he still wants me. Don't think I won't be a good wife, Roger, because I will. Better than I would have been before, much better. I won't cheat. I'll tell Paul the Rupert I knew was killed in the Spanish Civil War, shattered with a bullet in the stomach. It's true, isn't it? I'll tell him, about the last night we spent together before Rupert left for Spain. I'll tell him that too.'

'My God, what are you saying?'

'The truth, Roger.'

I put my arms around you but you were like a carving, unresponsive and cold. I wanted to look after you, protect you, take the whole of your burden onto my shoulders. I begged to do so.

'We'll manage together,' I said. 'We can travel in Europe. Then after – we'll settle somewhere. We'll be together. I'll never marry.'

You broke away from me, tearless; a pale caricature of yourself.

'You should,' was what you said. 'People should marry. It's natural. I wish you were forced as I am, Roger. It would give you an anchor, something to look forward to, somebody else to think about.'

'We'd have each other.'

'A strange ménage, you and I and a child. I wouldn't do such a thing to a child. Paul loves me. I'll give him everything I've got, I'll make myself. I'll go on with Paul from where we were before, as if the rest was a dream.'

'It won't work. He won't want it that way.'

'I hope he will, I have to hope. I'm not dead, am I? I'm not dead.'

And you went upstairs and began to pack and I sat in front of Maria's portrait, hating Rupert Augustinian. I couldn't even kill him. You can't kill a man already dead, even though the woman you love is nursing him back to health and your sister running away to bear his child.

You were right. Paul Martine did want you. You made him happy. When he wrote me from North Africa before he went into action he asked me to watch over you and Helena if he didn't get back to you. He told me how happy you made him.

'To be with her has been everything,' were his words. You let him name Helena after his mother. Even his mother loved you. You have always had two shares of love, your own and mine.

You are right. I am a fool. But not a greater fool than you, for you and you alone have precipitated what is about to happen. Tonight I am going to kill Rupert Augustinian. I will, of course, dispense with myself as well. It is for this reason I am writing to you. I shall address this letter care of Wilton, who has taken up what appears to be permanent residence in my house. As I sit at my desk under Maria's portrait he sits in my drawing room guarding Helena, who refuses to go to bed. With true British courtesy Wilton has excused me to attend to various business matters; putting my affairs in order before my arrest in the morning is probably the presumption under which he labours. No doubt he expects me to attempt an escape in the small hours of the morning, for Ferguson has placed himself near the door where he can observe without being seen. Wilton made no move to return with Helena to the hospital, as he promised Thomas, but he has ascertained by telephone that Augustinian remained with Thomas. Which Augustinian will do, of course, until Thomas sleeps, and the guard has supped on drugged coffee and the hospital rests in the peace of night.

There were a number of things I wished to do before I wrote this letter. I had the satisfaction of firing Joe Osman, my chauffeur, who had, as Wilton anticipated, returned Helena to this house after her visit to Maria. I had already dispensed with the man who was foolish enough to hide Thomas with a relation of his in Galata.

My personal properties are already entirely willed to Helena, in whom, paradoxical as it may seem, I seem to inspire at present the degree of compassionate fear which is usually conferred on a madman. Nevertheless, as my heir she will remember me with kindness. Time will remind her that she owes everything, even her education and Thomas, to me.

I think I was never more sane in my life. I was born in this house and I have every intention of dying in it. Certainly the last thing I intend to do is escape.

If I have any regret it is surely a minor one; that you, instead of your daughter Helena, should be here tonight when I welcome Rupert Augustinian. I have no doubt he will come. To protect Helena he will not be able to help himself. I would like to spare Helena. My hope is that she will sleep. It may be some consolation for you to know that you have passed on to Helena this indefinable quality that makes not only Thomas but also Wilton and Osman, not to mention Rupert Augustinian, her devoted slaves. Yes, even Osman. It was for Osman's benefit and certainly not Wilton's that I threatened Helena tonight, 'If I find out that you went to the house of Augustinian of your own free will, I will kill you.' Then I told Osman to get out and he went. Straight to tell Augustinian, of course, for that is what he is: Augustinian's spy, Augustinian's servant, Augustinian's slave.

I have never had a servant who loved me. One by one, after you left they went away, all the family retainers whom I had supported since Mother's death. They missed you. They didn't want to work for me. When you wouldn't come back I had to change the whole house. Your shadow sat on every chair, reminding me that all the love since we were children had been for you. The friends who called came only to enquire out of love for you and pity for me. During the war even the remaining fell away. But I had found a way of getting money to build the business again and when acquaintances cultivated me for financial gain, I was not deceived.

Then I wrote that I was the loneliest man in the world but still you would not bring the child and come back. A war widow, you preferred to go with a wastrel to China rather than return to the house of your birth. You let me come to London to beg you to return when the fool left you, but I found you had others to love you, small boys to support as well as Helena. You laughed all the time in that horrible place you lived in and I was ashamed for Helena. But you would not come back and I hated your laughter and your beauty and your wasted life and your friends and returned alone again.

'Why ever don't you marry, Roger?' you asked me, time and again. 'You really ought to marry. It would make all the difference to you.'

You were sorry for me. Even when you had scarcely enough to eat you were sorry for me. But not sorry enough to come back; not sorry enough to do what I asked.

You let me give advantages to Helena. Good Uncle Roger. Kind Uncle Roger. Dear old Roger! As I had been as a child, as a young man following my sister around as part of her court, paying her bills, entertaining her guests.

'She is going to be lovely, Roger,' Mother said. 'Look after her.'

How? When you wouldn't have me, lived as far away from me as you could get, refused every comfort I offered? You would never take advice or admit any measure of control over your actions. A woman of incredible whims, you moved like the wind without any sound direction. Just so long as you were moving.

'Forget the past, Roger. Get away from it. It's finished. Let it go.'

You could, but I can't. It is all I ever had. There was Mother; she died. There was you; Rupert Augustinian took you. There was Maria and she took Augustinian.

I might have forgotten Maria but for you. But the last offer I made you was no different from the first. You could have had with me everything a woman could want: security, a beautiful home in a city I know you love. And surely the last time I asked you it could be said that you had tried everything else. You wanted marriage, you had tried it twice. You had three children, two boys and Helena. You had tried working, you had tried starving, you had travelled, you had stayed still in one place. People, the friends that surround you, you would have had here as well as anywhere else. Certainly more so than you have in Cypress. Yet you preferred to involve yourself with a teacher who can scarcely provide for the children he has. You preferred him to me. You humiliated me for the final time. The house is empty of you forever. Every inch of the property and of our father's business is legally mine, willed to Helena and her heirs, providing none of it is shared with you, who would share nothing with me. You inherited all the physical attractions our family had to offer. That is all you inherit. Helena shall have the rest and will live rich enough to despise poverty. No other woman could be like you and resist wealth. This night will fade from Helena's mind, she will remember me with the compassion due to a benefactor and will in time look upon you as the fool.

I will seal this letter. The hour grows late and I face the door through which I am sure Augustinian will come. It is not his way of late to enter by a front gate. There is only silence in the drawing room. It is possible Helena and her guardian Mr Wilton have found themselves able to sleep.

A Letter from Osman

Madam.

The final word is kinder from the voice that is unfamiliar. This wisdom is not of my simplicity but by instruction of Augustinian. I am but the extra eyes, the third ear, the feet in the city, and now with honour, the hand of the master of this house. Peace be upon him, for he is good who rests his wracked body in sleep within two lengths of my arm.

Words write as snails crawl in the language comprehended but not of the mother tongue. You will forgive the frame of that which I record, knowing that the strength of my usefulness to the house of Augustinian abides in the exact truth of recollection, the reflection of sight to be recalled as a face in a mirror. I do not forget. By memory alone my race has survived.

I am Osman Josepian, an Armenian, whose parents were of the massacre, whose bones were succoured in the house of Augustinian, the milk of whose heart is of this house.

You, Madam, who know me not, must forgive me the sin of unknowing, for it was I, Osman, who now records the end, who was alas the messenger of the beginning who delivered into your hands at the house of Atherton, the letter of Augustinian, even as it was I, Osman, disguised as an Anatolian peasant, who drove the slow wheels of the hay wagon that brought from the world of death the shattered manhood of Augustinian and the sightless face of the dancer Maria Velasquez across the Spanish border. There were times, under that moon, when the work

85

of my hands and head held life and death in one skin, like twins in the womb, for I returned to Galata with only the courage of the spirit and the pride of Augustinian. The rest which had been offered to you in love was unworthy. The blessing of God rest upon you Madam, the beauty of your heart held in balance the weight of the years of sorrow, to be redeemed by the child of your heart and Augustinian's.

The work of the house of Augustinian has been my constant trust and the measure of my fidelity. Hunger wracked my belly and thirst my throat for the years of the war and the torture. There was no crack in the city that failed to hide my trembling, no doorway too narrow to enter, until the peace swept the city into sanity again. You will understand, Madam, that it was only when the nights were for sleep, the days for the regulated pulse of remunerative toil that I spoke to my friend and master, Augustinian.

'The house of Atherton, where once you sent me before the troubles blackened the face of Europe, seeks one who will drive. For me it is work of my choice, for I know the city. Will I go, now you no longer have special need of me and peace envelopes this house?'

The eyes of Augustinian rested on my face for many turns of the clock. 'Go,' he said then. 'Go, for independence is good, but do not tell the Spanish lady of this house, lest the memory of the house of Atherton disturb her sleep. There will come the time when I will reveal your occupation, should it be to your advantage to stay. It is long since one from this house entered the house of Atherton. To the master of that house, go as a man from Idirna, without mention of the house of Augustinian.'

The employment was good, Madam; the remuneration generous, the accommodation comfortable, the leisure adequate. The house of Atherton was formal and regulated. No guests came uninvited or stayed past the appointed hour. The play of diverse character that invigorates was absent. There was only one will in the house of Atherton, one order to obey without question or consideration. It suited me well, Madam, my tired limbs drove in luxury from one given point to another, no decision was required of me. My mind lay dormant, beneath the exchange of courtesies with merchants. My leisure was at the disposal of Augustinian, but he required of me no more than friendship.

It will not surprise you, Madam, that I grew fat and comfortable in the service of your brother's house until the day your daughter ran from me at Ayub and the duty of my heart conflicted with the work of my hands for bread.

On that day, before the drive began, I saw in the room that holds the portrait of my lady Maria, a girl whose hair was aflame, sparking into fire a silent house. With Mr Atherton, my duty as chauffeur was defined. With this girl a passenger in my car, my duty became confusion. She matched her wits against my orders, breaking my comfortable defence, Madam, my cocoon of non-identity, to address me with respect to my dignity of person as Mister Osman. Thrown suddenly on my guard, she forced me to the mental discipline of fitting fragments that my eyes had seen and my ears heard until the book was opened and I, Osman, called Joe the Armenian, found my name written upon the first page and the last. I remembered your light foot on the stair of the house of Atherton and how, when I placed in your hand the note, you smiled and enquired if I had time to wait. You tore open the envelope, Madam, and I turned my face away from your eagerness, remembering the eyes of Augustinian when he put the letter into my hand. The paper fell from your fingers to flutter like a dying bird at my feet. I stooped to retrieve it, Madam, but you swept it up and as we rose together you threw your hair back from your face and smiled again, dismissing me. 'Thank you. There's no reply.'

That courage, Madam, your hair, your daughter's hair. These were the first fragments I pieced together driving back from Ayub, myself once again Osman Joespian under instructions of Rupert Augustinian, only this time with the eyes of Augustinian more baffled than my own and the eyes of your daughter, Madam, like two bright stars after a sudden storm.

Driving back from Ayub, I became a man divided between heart and hands, my brain leapt with agility in the effort to build a bridge. For I saw the end of my years of comfort in the house of Atherton. My instruction had been to drive Miss Helena to Ayub for the view of two waters, with loss of employment if her foot left the car, which it had in a swift race to Rupert Augustinian. When there is conflict between food and heart there is only the acceptance of starvation. I knew that my heart was the heart of the house of Augustinian.

Last night was the last I spent in the house of Atherton. It was then that I looked with unveiled candour upon my employer's face and saw the seeds of madness engendered by fear and hate overtake his eyes like olives swollen to split. The life of your daughter was threatened, which sent me like an arrow in the night to find Augustinian, for well I knew how the heart of Augustinian quickened with new love for the one who is your daughter.

I came back with Augustinian and the lady Maria to the house of Atherton by the gate on the hill. The step of the lady Maria was light and taut as a wire spring walking between us under her black cloak. Three cats, we went softly from the gate down the garden wall, past the kitchen. As shadows go we approached the door that opens from the library. Our feet slipped onto the wood of the verandah and saw the door was open, showing a pale triangle of light from the desk lamp over the head of Roger Atherton.

'Si, si, let me go in now,' whispered my lady Maria Augustinian. We stepped up and she tapped this door. In shadow we waited.

'Come in, Rupert,' said the voice of Atherton. 'I am expecting you. The door is open.'

'Roger, it is I, Maria!'

'You!' the word was sudden cold rain. 'You, he sent you!' Then his voice screamed loud like the night-hawk. 'It's a trick. Come out, Augustinian. Come out like a man!'

Rupert Augustinian moved behind the lady Maria and helped her in through the door. Roger Atherton watched but did not move from behind his desk under the portrait of Maria, the dancer. Flying like a moth to the flame of the voices from across the salon, Helena was restrained at the door to the library by the hand of Mr Wilton. Struggling, she watched her uncle, waiting with controlled menace in front of his masterpiece. Pointing his revolver straight at my lady Maria, which of course she could not see, Roger Atherton spoke.

'Get out of my way, Maria.'

'For what reason, Roger? I have just come.'

'Long enough you hide behind Maria's skirt, Rupert Augustinian. Stand out!'

Into the silence that did not breathe a car growled to a halt and there was running in the street.

'Put that gun down, Atherton,' Mr Wilton commanded, his voice brittle and distinct, while his hand gripped the arm of your daughter like steel.

'Don't move, Wilton, if you value your life. Get back into the drawing room with Helena. For the last time, I ask you to go with them, Maria.'

The deep, full voice of Augustinian filled the room with awe and splendour, 'What do you want of me, Roger, that you offer me the release of death?'

It was then I saw the small hands of the lady Maria gripped tight behind her in the robes that clothed Augustinian and that the weight of her body pressed backwards against the weakness of his limbs, which were less than limbs, forcing him powerless to move. I heard her cry out. 'Kill me, whom you hate, Roger. Kill me who deceived you if you must kill, but spare Rupert, for the mercy of God!'

'Do you think I would arrange this meeting with one bullet in my gun? Look at me, Maria, the man who once loved you, whom you know well. Look at me now and you will know, three bullets are as easy to fire as one.'

Then the tongue of your daughter, which had been strangled in fear, flew loose like a coiled spring and filled the room.

'Thank God she cannot look at you, Uncle Roger. Thank God she is blind. To save him I see her little hands holding his clothes so that he, a cripple, cannot move. Kill me, Uncle Roger, instead of my mother, which is the same thing. Three bullets for our family. Wipe us out whom you have blighted, but not Maria, whom you once loved and who is blind, and Rupert Augustinian whom she loves.'

I am sorry, Madam, that I must inform you that the mind of Roger Atherton had already departed.

'You lie, Helena,' he screamed and swung the gun towards her. 'You mock me and you lie!'

Like the sound of the sea, the voice of Augustinian swelled into the air. 'In the young is truth, Roger. When I returned from Spain I was no longer a man and Maria was blind. For spies there is no quarter yet death is not granted until the course is run. We made one life from two fragments and now have tasted the reward. Helena is to me fulfilment and to Maria new sight. You are too late, Roger, no bullet can deny us this truth.'

But even by the voice of Augustinian, Madam, your daughter would not be saved, would not be still. Neither she nor her uncle heard the scuffling at the door that arrested the ears of others.

'I know the truth, Uncle Roger,' Helena cried. 'It is Mother you want to kill. You have always wanted to control her to make up for Maria. But she would not be controlled so you have tried to hurt her through me. You have failed. I found my father. I found him and I love him.'

Your brother did not heed if he heard the increased scuffling in the hall. The gun was steady in his hand and his eyes darkened upon your daughter even as I released Augustinian to get past him through the door, and the young man with the bandaged head flung himself in to fall upon the gun, and Mr Wilton knocked your daughter to the floor as the shot was fired. Such is always the thin, frail timeline of tragedy.

Perceive now, Madam, why I, Osman who was first was last. No one saw your brother go but I, who had lived longest in the house since the days of your presence. I, who had been a servant in the house lifted my eyes from the fainting form of the lady Maria to the portrait of her greatness on the wall and saw it move. Like a hound, I leapt over your daughter, Madam, and, followed by a man called Ferguson, who had unsuccessfully tried to restrain at the door the entry of the young man

Thomas, I went through the salon, the hall, and up the stairs to the room that was your brother's and threw myself upon the door – for I alone knew the secret stair hidden behind the portrait of the Spanish dancer.

Death, Madam, when the time is right has the speed of wings. I was too late. Even as I entered there was a second shot from within the room, which was as it had to be. Death is without strangeness to me and I looked upon your brother's face and knew the madness had left him with the final courage.

The house of Atherton is closed, Madam. Your daughter abides in the house of her father. On the afternoon of this day I drove her to the hospital that once again restrains, this time in docility, the activity of the one who will be the guardian of the heirs of Augustinian. After the seven days required by the dictates of those who practice medicine, leave will be granted to your future son and he will return with your daughter to the sanctuary of the home that you bless.

Augustinian will continue to honour this house with the wisdom of future years. No bullet can harm the limb of either bone or flesh that was thrown as a shield between your daughter and death. Once, in a time of intolerable disaster, Augustinian offered to me a quotation he had learned from the lips of his mother, peace be upon her, who spoke with your tongue:

'Joy is too exquisite, sorrow too bitter to be borne alone.'

You are not alone, Madam, the company of your heart is great. May I, Osman Josepian, the Armenian, be of that company. God's blessing rest upon the children of your flesh.

Peace be upon you.

In Conclusion, Mr Wilton

Dear Madam,

Thank you for your prompt reply to my letter marked 'Urgent'. As you so aptly remark, the use of the diplomatic bag for the safety of personal letters is categorical. Nevertheless, I can scarcely do otherwise than use it to conclude a correspondence which is, perhaps, the most unusual I have encountered in the course of my duties.

You will realise, of course, that I will be forced to reprimand severely the officer in the service who obliged you with the use of diplomatic facilities in the first instance. I refer of course to the original letter he allowed you to send to your future son-in-law in respect to Rupert Augustinian. Whereas from your point of view it appeared a normal request to make when you wished a completely private letter to reach a member of the diplomatic corps, our officer overstepped his authority in granting your request. As both he and your future son-in-law are contemporaries in age and experience, I am sure we can count on the fact that neither of them will ever be tempted to overestimate their privileges in the future. I have taken the responsibility of allowing the enclosure of the attached private letters to you in order that you may have a complete record of events as seen by the interested parties.

Your daughter Helena has entrusted to me the longest letter, most of which she had already written to you before the end of the affair.

I now proceed to the business of this letter which, from my point of view, must be written in order to supply the details that will conclude this affair officially.

The letter you sent to Thomas Pringle in the first instance was detached from the diplomatic bag before it was returned to me under circumstances which were, to say the least, peculiar. The copy of this letter, which you were wise enough to retain and therefore able to send to me and which I hereby return to you, supplied me with sufficient information to solve the mystery of your daughter and Rupert Augustinian. Your letter asked Thomas to make enquiries as to whether a certain Rupert Augustinian was still resident in Istanbul and, if so, would he inform you immediately so that you could write a note to introduce Helena. On the first consideration this would seem a simple and natural request, especially as you explained that your brother had never liked Augustinian and therefore it seemed foolish to consult him in the matter, at least until you were sure Augustinian was still in the city. Further consideration of your letter, however, would lead one to wonder why you did not tell Helena about Augustinian before she left you and suggest she find out about him from Thomas and not her uncle. More than this, you yourself having lived during your youth in the city would have acquaintances through whom you could have made enquiries had the matter not been of a highly personal nature. Obviously you were secretive because of your brother, which implied his more than casual interest in Augustinian.

You inform me now that you wrote to your brother five days before Helena left Cypress asking if Rupert Augustinian was still alive. You received a one-word answer by telegram – 'No'. This cryptic, brother-like message angered you into suspicion, especially as two days later a letter arrived from your brother in which he threatened to disinherit Helena if you breathed to her a word about the existence, past or present, of Rupert Augustinian. You replied to your brother with a telegram in kind, one word again, 'Fool', which seems, to say the very least, a rather indiscreet communication coming from a lady of your standing to a gentleman of your brother's wealth and promise in respect to your daughter's future. It could be surmised that you sadly underestimated the possible reaction your telegram might cause and allowed your daughter to follow it to Istanbul, apparently on the assumption that her engagement to a member of the diplomatic corps and her own high degree of personal integrity was adequate protection from the intrigues for which this city has been famous (from time immemorial). But as you were born in Istanbul and had yet refused to return here for twenty years, I was forced to wonder if the opposite applied. Did you overestimate the effect the telegram would have upon your brother? Did you hope, perhaps, to shock him into a recognition of life as it is now rather than as it was twenty years ago?

It has become apparent to me that you were willing to undertake certain risks in order to point out to your brother that you consider higher values exist for your daughter than those accruing to financial gain and comfort. Your daughter has been brought up in particular circumstances. She has now chosen the adult life she desires for herself through marriage to Thomas Pringle. Though you yourself might well suffer, you decided your daughter had the right to base her future on truth. Your brother stood between you and the telling of that truth and I find, Madam, that I am unable to offer condolences. For most of your adult life it appears from this correspondence you have borne the burden of a jealousy that you must have found intolerable and the removal of which will be to you an immeasurable relief. As it has been my privilege as well as my duty to read this correspondence, I take it upon myself to suggest that you merely precipitated an inevitable catastrophe. I do not agree with the Armenian, Osman. Insanity is not evident, but only one aspect of human passion which, unfortunately, is present in every member of the human race, but which in this case was remorselessly cultivated and selfishly harboured with intent to deny you your inheritance through the person of your own daughter. This has become obvious to me in the arbitrary disposal of property to which you have an equal right from birth. It is possible that since your first marriage, you have been unable to bring yourself to claim that which, in the view of any court, was your own. I beg of you to distinguish between legal right and generosity and feel free to accept the suggestion your daughter will put to you, remembering that she has now entered into her rightful inheritance as the heir of Augustinian.

You have, through your own integrity, brought up a daughter who will be of inestimable value as the wife of a member of the diplomatic service. I have no doubt that with her capable assistance, Thomas Pringle will ultimately occupy a post more distinguished than mine. This is, of course, a personal conjecture beyond my official capacity. Discretion is, without question, a most useful attribute of success and both your daughter and her fiancé have had the value of it indelibly impressed upon them.

Contrary to my expectations, I have enjoyed this correspondence as a revelation of human personality rarely revealed.

It is for this reason I send you these letters, covered by my own. I will be grateful for your acknowledgment of them as soon as time permits. The use of the ordinary mail, preferably airmail, will reach me, I trust, with greater directness than the vicissitudes of the diplomatic bag.

To conclude this correspondence, may I say that it will give me considerable pleasure to be informed in the not too distant future of your arrival in Istanbul. My car and the chauffeur I have recently engaged will be at your disposal for the duration of your visit.

I am,

Most respectfully yours,

WILTON

oooOOOooo

ABOUT THE AUTHOR

Kathryn Purnell was born in Vancouver, Canada in 1911. She travelled by sea to Australia with her family as a young woman. During the voyage she met and later married Australian scientist William (Bill) Purnell.

Kathryn embodied the soul and spirit of a creative writer. She maintained an intense interest in everything around her, the natural and spiritual worlds, the everyday and the eternal, diverse countries and their cultures, as well as the human condition (of which she had an uncanny understanding). A gifted educator, she was an inspiration to many aspiring writers to whom she taught creative writing. She believed intensely in the need to encourage women writers, the constraints on whom she felt herself at a very personal level.

Bill Purnell's work in the early years of UNESCO as head of its Science Cooperation Division took Kathryn to Paris to live in the immediate post war years, then to Cairo and later Jakarta. She travelled widely in Europe and later spent time in South Africa. Her husband's ill health compelled the family to return permanently to Australia in the late nineteen fifties, It was particularly in this period of her life, with the common pressures of maintaining a family, supporting a husband in his professional life and finding time to create, that she felt most strongly the constraints and limitations placed on the female creative spirit by the societal practices and beliefs of the time.

But create she did, both poetry and prose work. She also spent much of her time teaching aspiring writers, mostly women. Active in the Society of Women Writers, in 1998 she won The Alice Award, a biennial award for long-term and distinguished contribution to literature by an Australian woman. Other awards included the State of Victoria Short Story Award and the Moomba Short Story Prize both in 1966/67 and The Society of Women Writers Poetry Prize in 1972. In addition to poetry, Kathryn left a fine legacy of prose writings, much of it unpublished. A current project seeks to redress this by publishing some of her novellas, short stories and her singular novel.

ALSO BY KATHERINE PURNELL

PROSE
In an Urban Forest
Honey Eyes
Apollo in January
Sam in July

POETRY
Safari
Pandora
Harpsichord of Water
Otway Country
Fairy Trees: Poems for the Fitzroy Garde

www.ingramcontent.com/pod-product-compliance
Lightning Source LLC
Chambersburg PA
CBHW070631120726
47909CB00004B/1388